Mills & Boon Classics

A chance to read and collect some of the best-loved novels from Mills & Boon — the world's largest publisher of romantic fiction.

Every month, four titles by favourite Mills & Boon authors will be re-published in the *Classics* series.

A list of other titles in the *Classics* series can be found at the end of this book.

Rachel Lindsay

CASTLE IN THE TREES

MILLS & BOON LIMITED
LONDON · TORONTO

All the characters in this book have no existence outside the imagination of the Author, and have no relation whatsoever to anyone bearing the same name or names. They are not even distantly inspired by any individual known or unknown to the Author, and all the incidents are pure invention.

The text of this publication or any part thereof may not be reproduced or transmitted in any form or by any means, electronic or mechanical, including photocopying, recording, storage in an information retrieval system, or otherwise, without the written permission of the publisher.

This book is sold subject to the condition that it shall not, by way of trade or otherwise, be lent, resold, hired out or otherwise circulated without the prior consent of the publisher in any form of binding or cover other than that in which it is published and without a similar condition including this condition being imposed on the subsequent purchaser.

First published 1958
This edition 1980

© Scribe Associates 1958

Australian copyright 1980
Philippine copyright 1980

ISBN 0 263 73257 6

Filmset in 10 on 11 pt Plantin

*Made and printed in Great Britain by
C. Nicholls & Company Ltd
The Philips Park Press, Manchester*

CHAPTER ONE

WITH a sigh of relief Stephanie North put the cover on her typewriter, pushed back her thick red hair and walked through the outer office to a glass-fronted door marked:

NORTH & HARBOARD
INTERIOR DECORATORS

An elderly man seated behind the desk looked up as she came in. "Don't bother to wait for me, dear. I've got to go through these contracts before I leave."

Stephanie perched on the arm of her father's chair. "I'll give you a hand, Dad. You look tired."

"I'm fed up – not tired." He sighed heavily. "Two of my best men are off ill and then I get a letter like this." He picked up the sheet of notepaper in front of him and looked at the thin, spidery writing sprawled across it. "Ever heard of the Maroc Collection?"

"Who hasn't?" Stephanie grinned, for the Maroc Collection, comprising priceless jewellery and heirlooms of historic importance, was famous throughout the world.

She leaned over and picked up the letter, her curiosity stirring as she saw it was headed "Castelo de Arvores" and was signed by the Condesa de Maroc herself. The contents were short and to the point, requesting them to submit an estimate for redecorating the main rooms in the castle. She put down the letter and leaned forward to take a cigarette from a box on the table.

"We've never had a job like this, Dad. It could be the biggest thing we've ever done."

"I know." Mr. North rubbed the side of his nose. "What I

can't understand is why she should come to me when there are so many better-known firms."

"Perhaps she's looking for a bargain! You know what these rich old women are like. It would be tricky working in Portugal though, wouldn't it?"

"Not necessarily. Once we'd got out the plan of decoration, we'd hire a Portuguese firm to follow it through. Oh well . . ." He shrugged. "With Robson and Hawkins away I'll have to write and tell her it's impossible."

"You can't do that!" Stephanie exclaimed. "What about me?"

"Don't start that again," her father said impatiently. "I've told you a hundred times I won't send you on any more jobs."

"Then I don't see why you bothered to let me train as an interior decorator in the first place." She moved round the desk and flung herself in the chair opposite, her face so pale with anger that her hair glowed vivid red. "I'm fed up pounding a typewriter. If you won't let me go out on a job I'll hand in my notice."

"Hoity-toity!" her father answered. "There's no need to lose your temper."

"There doesn't seem any other way of making you understand I'm not a child! I'm twenty-two and it's time I made something of my life."

"Marry Robert. He's been nagging you long enough."

"I don't want to marry *anyone*. I want to—"

She choked on the words and Mr. North looked at her and sighed. Ever since she had left art school she had begged him to send her out on a job. The first time he had done so it had ended in disaster, for when the client had casually disregarded all her laboured designs, Stephanie had flung her pad in the woman's face and walked out. Twice she had been given another chance, but each time her temper had got the better of her until finally he had decreed that his daughter should be kept as far away from his clients as possible.

"It's the red hair, of course," he thought ruefully. But

temper did not get you anywhere in business and until Stephanie learned to control it she was better off in an office.

"You needn't look at me like that," Stephanie said suddenly. "I know you're thinking of all the jobs I mucked up, but I'm older now – it's been two years since I've done anything except shorthand and typing." She leaned forward. "Come on, Dad. Give me another chance."

"I can't. It's a big commission and if I accepted it I couldn't let them down."

"I *wouldn't* let you down, Dad – I promise."

"You say that every time. But when you lose that temper of yours—"

"I won't! I swear I won't! Please, Dad, I've so many wonderful ideas." She clasped her hands. "I can just see that castle! The large rooms and high ceilings, the mosaics and tapestries, the priceless carpets. These people must be worth a fortune – money would be no object. Dad, you've *got* to let me go!"

Father and daughter looked at each other in silence. The small glass clock on the mantelpiece chimed six and outside in Kensington High Street a car hooted and went on hooting.

Mr. North leaned back in his chair and sighed. "All right, you win. But I'm warning you, if you let me down on this I'll never give you another chance."

"Thank you, Dad!" Stephanie flung her arms round her father's neck. "You won't regret it."

Later that evening, as she walked with her father down the wide suburban road where they lived, Stephanie wondered how the neat little houses would compare to a Portuguese castle and mused on the fact that an old lady so many miles away could affect the lives of a family in England.

As they let themselves into the house the warm smell of baking filled the hall and Mr. North sniffed appreciatively. "Your mother's been making cakes today," he said.

Hearing voices, a middle-aged woman came into the hall. She was an older edition of Stephanie, her hair almost as red as her daughter's. "I was giving you another fifteen minutes," she said. "The supper's ready and Felicity's starving."

"You can say that again!" A slim girl put her head round the dining-room door and glanced at her sister. "You *are* late, though. What held you up?"

"I'll tell you over dinner."

In the dining-room talk was general and Stephanie nibbled a piece of bread and watched Felicity help her mother serve. Older than herself and far less vivacious, Felicity bore a strong resemblance to her father, with olive skin and dark hair that curled closely to her head. Considered the practical one of the family, she did not possess Stephanie's artistic flair, but in spite of this the two girls were excellent friends.

"Robert phoned just before you came in," Mrs. North said to Stephanie. "He isn't working late tonight after all, so he'd like to take you to a dance."

"I hope you didn't tell him I'd go!"

"Of course I did. I knew you weren't doing anything else."

"You might have asked me first."

"How could I when you weren't here? Anyway, it'll do you good to get out."

Stephanie shrugged. "It would if he didn't bore me stiff. You wouldn't like to go instead, would you Felicity?"

"I'm quite old enough to get my own dates, thank you," Felicity retorted, and walked out of the dining-room.

"What's the matter with her?" Stephanie asked in surprise. "Can't think why she's taken such a dislike to Robert. He's always polite to her."

"Perhaps that's the trouble," Mrs. North said. "I've often thought men treat Felicity as though she's their great-aunt."

Stephanie digested this in silence, but later, as she washed and changed, had to admit that there was some truth in the remark. But Felicity had only herself to blame that she had no man friend, for her sharp manner was more than enough to ward off any romantic-minded male. After all, how were they to know that her sarcastic tongue was only a cover for her shyness?

Still preoccupied with thoughts of her sister, Stephanie went downstairs to the lounge, where Robert Bryanston was waiting for her. A tall, heavily built man with a square chin and severe expression, his looks were not kind to him for, underneath his severe exterior, he was a sensitive if humourless person.

"How lovely you look!" he exclaimed as he took her hands. "I've never seen that dress before, have I?"

"Only a hundred times," she sighed, and drew her hands away as her mother and Felicity came into the room.

"How nice to see you, Robert," Mrs. North said. "Felicity, get Robert a drink."

Without a word Felicity moved over to the sideboard and came back with a glass of sherry. Robert took it and sat on the sofa.

"One day I'm going to ask for something different just to see the look on your face!"

"You'll never change," Felicity said calmly.

He smiled. "Aren't you going out tonight?"

"No. There's a programme on the radio I want to hear."

"Felicity doesn't go out enough for my liking," her mother interpolated. "She gets enough invitations, though. I'm sure I don't know why she keeps refusing them."

"Perhaps you're pining for a secret lover!" Robert grinned.

"I haven't got a secret lover and I can't stand men! Particularly those who don't know when to mind their own business." Scarlet with temper, Felicity ran out of the room and Robert looked so uncomfortable that Mr. North patted him on the shoulder.

"Don't take it to heart, old chap. I'm sure she didn't mean it. But it might be wiser if you and Stephanie pushed off before she comes down again."

A little later, as they sat at a table in a dimly lit restaurant while a band played softly from the dias, Stephanie studied

Robert and was honest enough to admit that, although he might not be her own personal ideal, he was far from unattractive. Indeed, if only his manner was as virile as his appearance she would have found him exceptionally interesting. Strange that some one so intelligent should be so hesitant in his approach. Yet he loved her and had been consistent in his attentions, taking her out as often as she would agree to go, sending her flowers and buying her gifts of chocolates and scent. Guiltily she wished she could return his affection and knew that if she could not do so it was only fair to stop seeing him. She wondered whether to tell him of her decision now or to allow her departure for Portugal to be the final break in their relationship. She was still pondering the question when he stood up and led her on to the dance floor.

Whatever else he might be he was certainly an excellent dancer, and moving round the room in his arms she gave herself up to the lilt of the music. Her steps fitted perfectly with his and he guided her so smoothly that she relaxed completely. What a pity they were not so well paired in life! But it was no good trying to force life into a pattern. One had to try and fit into the pattern that was presented to one.

It was not until they returned to their table that Stephanie told Robert that she was going to Portugal and outlined the offer that her father had received that day. If she had expected him to show enthusiasm she was disappointed, for he lit a cigarette and flung the match irritably into the ashtray.

"I suppose you're set on going?" he said at last.

"Of course. It's a wonderful opportunity for me."

"I don't suppose you'd consider it a wonderful opportunity to marry me instead?" He put his hand over hers. "Stephanie darling, you know how I feel about you. Why won't you marry me? Heaven knows I've asked you often enough."

"I don't love you," she said gently. "I keep telling you, but . . ." She stopped and looked at him beseechingly. "I wish you'd forget about me, Robert, and find someone else."

"You needn't tell me what to do with my life. You're the only girl I've ever wanted to marry, the only girl I've ever been in love with. I wish you'd give me a chance. You could still go to Portugal and we'd get engaged when you came back. Darling, please . . ."

"Robert, no! We've had all this out before so many times. You know how I feel – I like you, but not in the way you want."

"You'll be saying you'd like to be a sister to me next," he interjected bitterly. "All right, my dear. We won't talk about it any more for the moment. But don't think I've given up hope. I'll never do that until you're married to somebody else."

"Well, you needn't worry about my finding anyone in Portugal," she grinned. "I'm going there to work – and work exclusively."

"Wish I could be sure of that," Robert said glumly. "You know what these foreigners are."

"Oh, Robert!" Stephanie could not help laughing. "I'm sure they're no different from us. Anyway, the Portuguese are supposed to be very good-looking."

"Weedy little chaps with glasses, most of them."

"You're not putting me off at all. Think how thrilling it would be if they whispered sweet nothings in my ear with a broken accent!"

"If anyone's going to whisper in your ear it'll be me." He caught her hand again, his grip so painful that she realized it would be unwise to tease him further.

It was past midnight before he left her at the front door, and holding up her face to him she passively allowed him to kiss her. Although his hands were warm on her shoulders and his mouth ardent on hers, they evoked no response and she turned away quickly and inserted her key in the lock.

The house was in darkness and, switching on the light, she wandered into the kitchen to make herself a cup of tea.

Knowing her sister's habit of reading in bed, she put an extra cup on the tray and carried it upstairs.

A light was shining under the bedroom door and, tapping, she pushed it open and walked in. Felicity was lying in bed, her reading lamp on. With her face devoid of make-up and her hair tousled, she looked much younger than twenty-seven. There was a sad droop to her mouth that Stephanie had not noticed before, and in that moment of silence between them she knew there was something wrong. But Felicity was already sitting up, pushing the hair from her eyes and groping for her glasses.

"You're early tonight," she said calmly. "What's the matter?"

"I got fed up. Robert gets more boring by the hour."

"Only because you don't love him."

"It's not my fault." Stephanie put the tray on the bedside table. "I thought you might like a cup of tea."

Felicity took the cup and sipped, staring in front of her without a word. Stephanie sat on the edge of the bed, determined not to leave the room until she had discovered what was wrong.

"What's the matter, Lissa?" she asked, using the pet name which she called her sister in moments of affection. "You look as if you've been crying."

"Don't be ridiculous! I don't know what's the matter with you all this evening." Felicity gave a nervous laugh. "First Mother and now you. Really, Stephanie, aren't I old enough to have any privacy in my life?"

"I don't want to pry," Stephanie said quickly, "but there's so obviously something wrong. Robert wasn't right this evening, was he – about your being in love with someone?"

"It would be better if you and Robert paid less concern to my love life and concentrated on your own. You've no right to keep him on a string and he's a fool to let you."

"What a horrid thing to say! It's not my fault he won't take no for an answer."

"He would if you said it firmly enough."

"What more can I say except that I don't love him?"

Felicity shook her head and in the lamplight her glasses became opaque so that it was impossible to see the expression in her eyes.

"Glasses," Stephanie thought in annoyance, "can be as effective as window blinds."

"Perhaps I'd better be getting to bed," she said quietly. "I didn't come in here to quarrel with you."

"I'm sorry." Felicity set her cup carefully on the tray and lay back on her pillow. "I'm a beast to vent my temper on you. I think I must be working too hard. We're doing a new index for the library and it's pretty tiring."

"That's all right." Stephanie wondered if it were tiredness that was marking lines of strain on Felicity's face, but knew better than to question her sister further at the moment. Murmuring goodnight, she stood up and, yawning, closed the door behind her.

She was too tired to cogitate on Felicity's behaviour, but uneasiness lay in the back of her mind, ready to be brought out and thought over at a more opportune moment. Snuggling under the sheets she closed her eyes. What a day this had been! The chance to decorate a castle; her father's promise to let her go to Portugal; Robert proposing again. Poor Felicity! How dull her life was by comparison.

And Felicity, alone in her own room, was thinking exactly the same. How dull her life was and how dull she was herself. "Why should any man want you?" she thought miserably and, snatching off her glasses, set them down sharply beside her bed. Without them the room was blurred, the furniture indistinct, even her own reflection in the dressing-table mirror could not be discerned. She was a pale image, a ghost.

'I'm a ghost all right,' she thought bitterly. 'A pale facsimile of my sister.' What right did she have to expect any man to look at her when they could look at Stephanie instead? What a waste it was, she thought as she turned off the light. If only Robert had fallen in love with her, how gladly she would have accepted his proposal and how happy she would have made him. They both liked music, reading, and walking in the rain; they had so many things in common. Yet compared with green eyes and auburn hair, all this was unimportant. Sniffing miserably, Felicity pulled the sheets up close and tried firmly to think of the future and forget the might-have-been.

CHAPTER TWO

IN the days that followed Stephanie decided to find out all she could about the Maroc Collection and the Castelo de Arvores, which she learned meant "Castle in the Trees."

Wondering how best to do this, she decided to go through the files of a daily newspaper, and, one morning shortly after her father had written to the Condesa accepting the offer of work, she entered a long, low room in Fleet Street where the walls were lined with dozens of steel files.

A man in shirt-sleeves with two or three pencils stuck behind his ear led her over to a corner, deposited her on a high stool and dumped a foolscap folder in front of her.

"You'll find all you want there, miss," he advised her. "Take your time – there's no hurry."

Stephanie thanked him and settling down to her task, soon became engrossed. There were numerous photographs of the castle exterior and gazing at the grey turrets and dark façade, she wondered if the inside were as gloomy and forbidding. The old Conde, founder of the Collection, had died two years earlier, leaving a widow and two sons, and although there was not a lot of information to be gleaned from the newspapers, everything she read about the family increased her curiosity and made her long to meet them, especially the woman who signed herself: "Yours in confidence, Maria, Condesa de Maroc."

Suddenly Stephanie became aware of somebody watching her and, glancing up, saw a thin, fair-haired young man. He gave her an engaging grin.

"Don't mind me," he said. "You've got the file I'm interested in too. But go right ahead – I'm not in any particular hurry."

"I've finished anyway." Stephanie pushed the folder along the counter towards him.

"Thanks. Find what you want?"

"I wasn't looking for anything in particular," she said. "I just wanted to find out all I could about the Maroc Collection."

"Me too." He opened the file and she glanced at him surreptitiously as he began to look through it. Not more than thirty, with a thin, freckled face, candid grey eyes and light brown hair, his appearance had a boyishness belied by the assurance of his movements.

As if aware of her scrutiny, he turned his head and smiled. "I'm a writer," he said. "I bash out thrillers and I'm catching up on my knowledge of jewels and jewel collections."

"Well, you've certainly chosen the right one," she said. "The Maroc Collection's fabulous, I believe." Giving him a friendly smile, she turned to go. "Good luck with your search."

"Thanks." He rose politely from his seat, but before she had reached the office door was once more engrossed in the file.

It was a humid morning when Stephanie set out for Portugal. Although she had never flown before, the efficient and matter-of-fact atmosphere that pervaded the terminal hall at London Airport went a long way to allay her fears, and as she followed the other passengers through the Customs shed and out on to the tarmac, she experienced her first thrill of anticipation.

A gust of wind lifted her skirt and as she stooped to hold it down, another caught her hat. With an exclamation of annoyance she watched it bowl along the ground, coming to rest against the legs of a thin, fair-haired man some few yards behind her. He picked it up and held it out with a grin.

"Yours, I believe."

"Thanks. I didn't realize—" She stopped short and looked at him more closely.

At the same moment he smiled and held out his hand. "Hello! I thought I recognized you."

Stephanie shook his hand. "I never expected to see you here! Are you bound for Lisbon too?"

"Yes." They walked towards the plane that glinted silver in the early-morning sunshine and she preceded him up the ladder. He followed her along the aisle, hesitating as she sat down. "May I sit with you now that we're practically old friends?"

She laughed. "Of course. I'll be glad of your moral support – this is my first flight."

"I'd never have guessed it. I was just thinking what a very composed young lady you are."

No compliment could have pleased Stephanie more and she warmed to the young man. "I suppose you're going to Portugal for local colour for your book?"

"Right first time. My name's Johnny Carlton."

"I'm Stephanie North." He looked at her expectantly and she added, "I'm an interior decorator."

"Are you, by Jove? You don't look at all the type."

Her eyes crinkled. "What does the type look like, Mr. Carlton?"

His reply was forestalled by the revving of the engines and the stewardess walked slowly down the aisle handing out pieces of chewing gum. The plane taxied along the ground and with an imperceptible motion lifted into the air. Within a few moments the airport lay far below them and Stephanie relaxed and unfastened her safety-belt.

"I'm glad that's over – I was petrified."

"You didn't look it. You must be very good at hiding your feelings."

Stephanie laughed and as the plane droned over the south coast and across the shimmering blue sea, she told him something of her ambitions and her desire to prove to her father her ability as a decorator.

"You'll find it difficult getting some of your ideas accepted in Portugal," Johnny Carlton said. "I know the people there very well and believe me, they're more hidebound than anywhere else in the world."

"Don't say that!" she protested. "I'm simply bursting with ideas for the castle."

"The castle?" He sounded surprised.

"The Castelo de Arvores where the Maroc Collection is. That's why I was interested in those press cuttings. We've been commissioned to redecorate the castle and I wanted to find out all I could about it and about the Marocs before coming out here."

She was not prepared for the sharp intake of breath nor the strange expression that crossed his face as he spoke. "So you'll be staying there, then? You're a very lucky young lady. It's a difficult place to get into – they won't allow any sight-seers because of the Collection."

"I expect I'll see it for myself."

"I'd like to know what you think of it – it's supposed to be magnificent. And it would help me a lot with my story if I could find out something about it. I'm staying in Cintra, incidentally – it's the nearest village to the castle."

"I'm glad you'll be so close," she said involuntarily. "I've suddenly got cold feet about living with foreigners."

"There's nothing to be afraid of," he replied. "Come and see me any time you like. I'm at the village inn."

"I should like that." Stephanie turned to gaze through the window at the changing landscape below, and presently they touched down on the tarmac of Lisbon Airport.

They descended from the plane and to the accompaniment of excited voices and varied gesticulations, were escorted through the Customs and out to a row of taxis.

Johnny Carlton touched her arm. "Can I give you a lift?"

"I rather think I'm being met." She looked round doubtfully and a black-haired man in the uniform of a chauffeur came up to her.

"Mees North? I am from the Castelo de Arvores. Your luggage, please?"

Indicating the cases at her feet, Stephanie turned to the Englishman. "Perhaps I can give *you* a lift?"

"Not this time. I'll probably stop off in Lisbon and have

a look round. But don't forget to keep in touch with me."

With the promise that she would, Stephanie climbed into the back of the silver-grey Mercédès-Benz and waved through the window as they drew away from the kerb. It was a short drive to Lisbon and driving down its wide boulevards it was difficult to believe oneself so far from home. They did not slow their pace in the heavy traffic and several times she clenched her hands to prevent herself from crying out, but the little chauffeur was in magnificent control of the car and gradually her fears abated.

Lisbon behind, they drove through flat country and began to climb so leisurely that it was a surprise to look out the window and see the plains stretching below them. It was a landscape of sweeping downland starred with dwarf gorse and yellow irises, while directly in front rose the craggy hills of the Serra. The village of Cintra lay at its foot with sprawling houses half hidden by elms and the verdant green of lemon trees. There was a large, dusty square bounded on one side by the Royal Palace and on the other by the Central Hotel, which Stephanie guessed must be the inn where Johnny Carlton was staying.

The bonnet of the car turned towards a narrow road and they seemed to climb into the very heart of the mountain itself. Higher and higher they went until gradually the light faded as the tangled branches of trees twisted themselves together above them, turning the rays of the sun into translucent green light. Immense stones could be glimpsed through the heavy foliage, piled strangely one on top of the other as if they had been thrown there by volcanoes.

In and out the car twisted and Stephanie wondered whether they would ever reach the top. Almost as the thought entered her mind, the engine accelerated and with a burst of speed they turned the last bend and drove through massive gates into a wide, undulating driveway. Stephanie peered through the windscreen, catching her breath at first sight of the Castelo. It was darker and more forbidding than she had imagined, but set amongst the trees it had a strange enchantment in spite of its unyielding aspect.

As they sped through the grounds she recognized trees and plants from every part of the world: palms, bamboos, cedars of Lebanon, azaleas, giant fuchsias blooming with colour, and here and there clumps of rhododendrons and magnolias. They grew close to the very walls of the castle itself, softening the harsh grey stone and ugly outline of jutting turrets.

Under an archway they swept, drawing to a stop by an iron-studded door. Stephanie climbed up the steps but before she could lift the heavy knocker the door was opened by a tall, thin man in the livery of a butler. With the feeling that she was stepping back into the past, Stephanie entered a high-ceilinged hall with dark panelling and a black-and-white marble tiled floor. Without a word the butler ushered her into a large, empty room and she glanced round with interest. It was furnished in the French period: a delicate Aubusson carpet, worn threadbare in patches, yet still beautiful, covered the floor and standing on it were intricately carved sofas and chairs, all covered in faded needlepoint. Glass-fronted cabinets were placed in alcoves round the walls and inside them could be glimpsed porcelain and ivories with one or two unusual statues in jade and rose quartz. She moved nearer to study one of them, marvelling at the delicacy of design and workmanship.

"They are excellent, are they not?"

Stephanie swung around to see a silver-haired woman in a long black dress that covered her from her neck to the toes of her elegant pointed shoes.

"You are Miss North, I take it?" The voice was thin and soft with a faint accent. "I am the Condesa de Maroc. Sit down, child."

Stephanie did as she was told, a faint flush seeping into her cheeks beneath the intent gaze of the old lady.

"You are younger than I thought," the Condesa said finally. "When Mr. North wrote he was sending someone I anticipated an older person, a little more sophisticated perhaps."

"I know my job, Condesa," Stephanie said quietly. "Someone with sophisticated ideas might want to spoil your home."

"No one would be allowed to do that," came the sharp reply. "Many people have tried to mark their personalities on these rooms but all have failed." The white hands fluttered and there was a sparkle of diamond rings. "But it is wrong of me to condemn you because of your youth. Miguel would be annoyed if he could hear me. Miguel is my son," she explained. "It was he who persuaded me to have the Castelo renovated. There is a great deal to be done, as I am sure you will see for yourself."

"It seems magnificent to me."

"It *is* magnificent, but even so it can be improved. Much of the gold leaf on the carvings had faded, the curtains are badly worn, as you will see if you look at them closely, and damp has obliterated many of the murals. We want it all restored, made to look as it must have looked a hundred years ago." The Condesa stood up. "But I will not say any more. I will leave it to my son. He is better able to tell you what we require."

She crossed over to the marble fireplace and pulled at a tasselled bell. Almost before she took her hand away the door opened and the butler appeared.

"Dinis, tell my son I would like to see him."

The butler bowed and withdrew, and in a short space of time the door was swung open again and a young man came in.

"You sent for me, Mama?"

"Yes, Miguel. I want you to meet Miss North."

The man swung round, his expression changing comically. "Good gracious, you're only a child!"

Stephanie's eyes flashed and with an effort she held back the words rising to her throat. She was not so successful in controlling her expression, for the dark eyes watching her narrowed with amusement and the wide, thin mouth curved in a smile.

"Forgive me for being so rude. I can see I've annoyed you."

"Not at all," she replied. "But next time I take on a job I'll dye my hair grey!"

Miguel laughed. "I assure you there is no need. For the moment I was taken unawares, but I am certain you are as competent as you are lovely."

Stephanie bowed her head slightly in acknowledgement of the compliment, but her lips were still compressed in annoyance.

"You must be tired after your journey, Miss North," said the Condesa. "I suggest you have a rest and unpack. After tea Miguel will show you round the Castelo and tell you what he wants done. Meanwhile Dinis will show you your room."

Stephanie followed the butler up the mahogany stairway and at the top turned to glance back into the hall, surprised to see Miguel de Maroc looking after her. He lifted his hand in a gesture of favour and she was reminded of the portraits she had seen of Portuguese noblemen. At this distance the man looked handsome and commanding, for one could not see that the mouth was too thin, the dark eyes set a shade too close: one was only aware of the tall, thin frame, the delicate white hands and shining black hair. Replying to his gesture with a smile, she followed Dinis down the rambling corridor, through another *salon* filled with Victorian bric-à-brac and down a few stairs to what she recognized as the older part of the Castelo.

Pushing open a narrow teak door, the butler entered a bedroom. "Your cases are here," he said. "If there is anything else you require, please ring the bell."

The door closed behind him and Stephanie looked round, testing the bed with its overhanging drapes and running her foot across the wood floor, polished like glass. A Gothic window gave her a glimpse of the garden and terraces below and by craning her neck she could see in the far distance the estuary of the River Tagus.

Glancing at her watch, she saw there was plenty of time before tea and, tired after her journey, she decided to have a rest before washing. Slipping off her dress and shoes, she put on a housecoat and lay down on the opulent bed. She took up very little of its vast space and, lying relaxed on her back she let her gaze travel to the window again. A soft breeze rustled the tops of the trees and the blueness of the sky had an almost piercing quality, unlike the soft blue of the English summer skies. Portugal! she thought. Land of sunshine and mystery . . .

CHAPTER THREE

STEPHANIE wakened from her doze and frowned as she looked up at the ornate ceiling. She lay quiet for an instant and then as memory returned, yawned luxuriously and got to her feet.

She washed in the small bathroom which had been converted from a closet, changed into a fresh dress and walked back along the corridor. A journey which had seemed so simple when following Dinis now assumed formidable proportions, and for some time she wandered in and out of rooms and up and down corridors, never managing to find the main stairway, although it did afford her an opportunity of seeing the Castelo. Much of the furniture was inlaid with mother-of-pearl, forming intricate patterns on shining mahogany, and many oil paintings of Portuguese men and women lined the walls. But over all there was a smell of mustiness and damp, weighting the air and seeming to shimmer like a haze over the brocades and satins that hung stiffly across the windows.

She hurried down another few steps and walked into yet another ante-room. Certain that she had not seen this one before, she halted.

"I really am lost," she thought, and did not realize she had said the words aloud until she heard a voice behind her and, swinging around, saw Miguel de Maroc.

"Don't give up hope," he smiled. "The rescue party has arrived!"

"Thank goodness! I've been wandering about for ages trying to find my way downstairs."

"I'll have to give you a compass," he answered.

"Remember always work your way south-west. That's where the main stairway is. The rest of the Castelo branches off from that." He preceded her through the room and within a few moments led her out on to the Minstrels' Gallery. "You see," he said with a wave of his hand, "it's simple when you know the direction."

"As simple as the maze at Hampton Court," she answered drily.

He laughed and ran lightly down the stairs, pausing at the bottom to wait for her. She was half-way to meet him when he raised his hand and called out for her to stop. In surprise she did as he asked, flushing slightly at the intentness of his gaze.

"You may come down now," he called after a moment, and did not speak again until she was abreast of him. "You must forgive the abruptness of my request, but you looked so lovely against the panelling. Your hair is exquisite: such a magnificent Titian is rare in these days of dyed auburns. When I saw you coming down the stairs I realized how beautifully your colouring represents my home."

"Represents your home?" Puzzled, she echoed his words. "I'm afraid I don't understand you."

"Never mind," he said softly. "One day I will explain it to you. Now let us go and have tea. My mother is waiting for us in the *salon*."

They crossed the hall and Stephanie glanced through the half-open dining-room door, catching a glimpse of large bowls of flowers placed the full length of a long table and against one wall a trellis up which climbed thick green vines. She longed to stop for a moment, but her host was already at the drawing-room and she followed him in, smiling as she saw the Condesa seated in front of a table on which stood a silver tea-set.

With an inclination of her head the old lady indicated a chair and Stephanie sat down.

"What a beautiful dining-room you have," she remarked as she accepted her cup from the Condesa. "I glanced in on my way here."

"It is the only Portuguese room in the Castelo," the Condesa replied. "The rest of the house is middle European."

"I'm all for people furnishing their homes to suit the climate and the country," observed Stephanie.

"Then your English homes must be very dull!" Miguel de Maroc leaned forward, his chin resting on one narrow hand. "No matter where you live there's only one standard of beauty."

"But not everybody has the same standard," she demurred. "Your opinion might not be mine."

"For your sake I hope that is not true. Otherwise I would regretfully have to dispense with your services."

Stephanie turned scarlet and with an effort remembered her father's warning. She bent her head and sipped her tea, conscious all the time of the man watching her.

The Condesa turned to Stephanie. "After tea my son will show you over the Castelo and tell you his own suggestions."

"Thank you," Stephanie said coolly. "I am sure the Conde knows exactly what he likes."

The Condesa's spoon clattered in her saucer and carefully she steadied it. "My son the Conde is abroad."

Discomfited, Stephanie glanced at Miguel and he looked back at her, his face expressionless.

"I'm sorry to disappoint you, Miss North, but my brother is the head of the family now. I am the younger, insignificant son."

"I'm sorry. I took it for granted—"

"That is to be expected. Most people would assume that the Conde would be concerned with his home, but I am afraid it is left to me to restore it to its former beauty and grace. Carlos would see the walls fall down before he would touch them, would allow the brocades to rot and the furniture to crumble if it were not for me. If I could—"

"Miguel, please!" The Condesa's thin voice stopped the flow of words. "Miss North is not interested in our family concerns."

"You are right, Mama, I will remember."

Politeness forced Stephanie to behave as though she had not heard this conversation, but as she turned her gaze to the windows and looked through them to the sun-dappled lawns, her curiosity stirred and she puzzled over the possible significance of what had passed between the Condesa and her younger son. Miguel de Maroc had spoken with almost startling bitterness of his brother and Stephanie mused over the reasons for the animosity that evidently existed between the two men.

Her thoughts were interrupted by Miguel who, getting to his feet, made a slight bow in her direction. "If you are ready, Miss North . . .?"

Stephanie stood up and together they left the drawing-room to begin their tour of inspection. Listening to her escort recount the history of every piece of furniture and ornament, she was amazed at the difference in him, for he threw aside his armour of coolness and became passionately alive, vibrating with the force of his emotion. The furniture was real to him, the ornaments and paintings were full of colour and the fabrics that he touched were alive.

Stephanie knew the present Conde owned the Castelo and the Collection, and, her mind once more reverting to Miguel's conversation with his mother during tea, she wondered whether it rankled in Miguel's mind that all that he saw did not belong to him, and if this could be the reason for his bitterness towards his brother.

But she was left little time to think about it for there was so much to see and admire, so many of her guide's suggestions to discuss, and her own ideas to give expression to, that when they had completed the tour and returned to the hall, she felt herself swaying with fatigue.

With an effort she tried to shake off her tiredness and pay attention to what Miguel was saying.

"There are a great many things here that will remain untouched," he continued. "Most of the furniture is priceless, as I am sure you realize, but some of it is Victorian junk which my father never found time to get rid of."

"It's going to be expensive to do all the renovations you suggest."

"No doubt. But we are a wealthy family, Miss North. We have more money than you have ever dreamed of."

"I am sure you have," she said drily. "And you will need to use a great deal of it to put this place to rights."

"That is understood," he said loftily. "Now come, I will show you the library. You must be particularly careful with this room. It is my brother's special retreat, a holy sanctum where very few are allowed to go."

He pushed open a door and Stephanie entered an octagonal-shaped room which she guessed was built inside one of the turrets. Book cabinets were let into four walls while a large alcove in the centre of the fifth housed alabaster figurines. Indirect lighting accentuated the three-dimensional appearance, giving each statue a semblance of life that was beautiful and at the same time disquieting. Here the furniture was French Empire, heavy, sombre and obviously looked after with great care, while the windows were partially hidden by thick velvet drapes.

"There doesn't seem much wrong here," she remarked.

For answer he scraped his nail along one wall, and when he drew his hand away she saw gilt gleaming through the mark he had made.

"You see!" he said. "Some crass idiot has stained the woodwork. All this polish must be scraped away and the original colour restored. But we will talk about it later. You have been standing a long time and must be tired."

Surprised at his sudden concern, she admitted to a slight fatigue, and under the sympathy of his gaze, relaxed and leaned against a chair. "It must be the journey as well – I've never flown before."

"A drink will revive you. If you come to the *salon* as soon as you are changed I will mix you a Portuguese cocktail."

"Is that a promise?"

The thin mouth curved. "When you have tasted it you might consider it a threat!"

Stephanie was still smiling at the remark when some half-hour later she descended the stairs to the drawing-room. The green dress she wore was a perfect foil for her red hair and white skin and she was conscious of the Condesa's appraising glance as she came in.

"Sit down, my dear," said the Condesa. "My son will be here shortly and will give you some refreshment. You must be tired after your tour of the Castelo. Miguel can be an exhausting host."

"A little." Stephanie seated herself opposite the old lady and smiled. "But he's so enthusiastic that one can forgive him. He's obviously extremely interested in beautiful things."

"So are most men," the Condesa said drily, and looked at Stephanie again, her eyes travelling over her shimmering dress and the red hair that seemed alive in its brightness. "You are very lovely yourself, Miss North, but you do not need an old woman to tell you that."

Stephanie flushed slightly. "You're very kind."

"I am merely stating a fact. You will receive many compliments while you are here," the Condesa went on, but you will do well not to take them too seriously. Portuguese men worship beauty and, as you have already discovered for yourself, my son Miguel worships it more than most. However, I am sure that like all the English you are level-headed and do not need me to warn you not to let your heart get the better of your head."

Somewhat at a loss, Stephanie spoke carefully in reply. "I appreciate all you've said, Condesa. But I do not think I'm likely to need any warning."

"I am glad." The Condesa turned slightly in her chair. "If you would like to smoke, my dear, there are cigarettes in that box over there. I have never done so myself, but I know it is a habit increasingly adopted by young people today."

As Stephanie walked over to the table and took a cigarette, she pondered on the Condesa's remarks. How strange that the old lady should think it necessary to warn her against her own son! But little as she knew of the Condesa, she realized that pride of race was as much a part of her make-up as her silver hair and aristocratic nose. Following on this it was easy to deduce that she also laboured under a constant fear that her sons might make unsuitable marriages – and what could be more unsuitable than marriage to a foreign girl?

'How ridiculous!' Stephanie thought. 'My first day at the Castelo and I am warned against marrying the son of the house!'

"Are you expecting the Conde back soon?" she inquired as she took her seat again, cigarette in hand.

"I'm not sure. Not for several weeks anyway – so it is unlikely that you will be meeting him. I expect you will have finished your work and returned to England by the time he arrives home."

"Oh? What part of the world is he in?"

The Condesa turned her head restlessly. "It is very hot in here. I wonder if you would mind opening the windows wider?"

"Of course." Stephanie jumped to her feet and hastened to do as the old lady asked. "Do you feel faint? Can I get you anything?"

"No, it was just a passing dizziness. I am quite all right now."

"Forgive me for keeping you waiting."

They turned at the sound of Miguel de Maroc's voice at the door and the Condesa stretched out her hand.

"There you are, Miguel. We were wondering what had happened to you. Miss North is getting thirstier every minute."

Miguel stepped forward. "Forgive me, Miss North, but I am not used to young ladies who keep such good time! *You* are as punctual as you are lovely!" He turned to his mother. "There have been no red-headed women in our family, have there, Mama?"

"A long time ago there was," the Condesa said softly. "Your great-great-grandmother . . ."

"Of course, the lovely Isabelita. I was forgetting." He smiled. "Now then, Miss North, the drink I promised you."

He handed her a glass and Stephanie sipped, making a face as the fiery liquid trickled down her throat. She coughed and reached for her handkerchief as the tears started to her eyes. "Gosh, it's sharp! What's in it?"

"That's my secret," he replied. "But wait a few moments. The effect is exhilarating."

"Two of these would put me under the table!"

"I would never give you two. When one drinks too much it destroys the character." He lowered his voice, speaking so softly that she knew he did not want his mother to hear. "And you should always remain as you are – warm and vibrant and aware of everything around you."

Embarrassed, Stephanie put her lips to the glass and wondered how Miguel would behave on closer acquaintance if he were like this after twelve hours. Yet she would not have been human had she not been flattered by his attentions, and surreptitiously she studied him as he handed his mother a tall glass filled with fruit cup.

They had just finished their drinks when a gong rang through the hall and with a glance at his mother, Miguel stood up, gave her one arm and held out the other to Stephanie.

"I never keep meals waiting, Miss North. I can't bear food to be spoiled."

"My son is a gourmet," the Condesa said, and Miguel laughed.

"A gourmand too, Mama. I must watch my weight or I'll be getting fat!"

Even as he spoke Stephanie knew he did not mean what he said, for he glanced down at himself, obviously aware that he made a handsome figure in his black suit and white evening shirt.

The three of them walked into the dining-room and Stephanie thought again how beautiful it looked with the candles in their slim silver stands shedding their soft light over the polished wood of the table.

"Your son has put me on my mettle today, Condesa," said Stephanie as she seated herself and unfolded her napkin. "He knows as much about design and colour as I do."

"He is interested in such things," the old lady replied. "It would have made an excellent career for him."

Stephanie looked at Miguel curiously. "Why didn't you take it up?"

"A very good question, Miss North. But unfortunately one needs the time to do so and with Carlos away so much I have to be here to look after the estate."

"If I had a home like this I'd never want to be away from it."

"Unfortunately, my brother doesn't feel like that. As I told you, he finds outside things of far more interest than his own home. Sometimes I think he hates the Castelo."

"Miguel!" The Condesa's voice was sharp. "Please do not speak like that of your brother to strangers!"

For the first time the young man had the grace to look abashed. "I am sorry, Mama."

In the uncomfortable silence Stephanie glanced at her plate. The atmosphere of strain was so apparent that it seemed to hang like a pall over the room, putting an end to all conversation so that the dessert was finished in silence.

Almost as soon as Stephanie put down her spoon and fork the Condesa signalled the butler and pushed back her chair. She stood at the head of the table, seeming taller in the flickering light of the candles that flung her shadow on the wall.

"We will have coffee in the *salon*," she said quietly and led the way from the room.

In the elegant drawing-room the tension eased and as the old lady dispensed coffee from a hand-beaten silver pot, she chattered lightly for the first time, displaying unexpected charm.

"Do you have your coffee black or white, Miss North?"

"Black, please."

"Good. I always think milk spoils the taste." The Condesa passed her cup. "I hope you will find the food here to your liking. Many English people find it too highly seasoned."

"I'm sure I'll like it," Stephanie smiled. "The dinner was excellent."

"So it should be," Miguel laughed, "considering we have a first-class French chef."

"Then in that case I'm certain I won't have any complaints. French cooking is universally appreciated." She turned back to the Condesa. "I can see I'll have to be careful while I'm here. Staying at your lovely house will make me feel as if I'm taking a holiday instead of working."

"I hope it *will* be a holiday for you," the Condesa said graciously. "There are many lovely walks you would enjoy. And if you need the car at any time you have only to say so. We are a little way from the sea, but it would be well worth your going down for a day."

"I'd love that. But I've made up my mind not to do any sightseeing until I've broken the back of the work here." She put down her cup. "Your son has asked me to start with the library."

"The library!" The old lady's voice was startled and the delicate Sèvres cup on her hand rattled against the saucer as she looked at her son. "You gave me your promise, Miguel, that you would leave the library alone."

"I didn't promise, Mama, and you must realize for yourself that we can't do up the rest of the Castelo and leave the library untouched."

"It's out of the question. Carlos will be angry."

"I can't help that." His reply was cold and emphatic. "Miss North will start on the library tomorrow."

"She certainly won't!" A deep voice echoed across the room and with a start the three occupants turned to look at the tall, black-browed man standing at the door. Slowly he advanced into the room and Stephanie knew without question that this was the master of the Castelo. Arrogance was in

33

every line of his face, in the wide shoulders, the haughty carriage of head, the intense black eyes and narrow, bitter mouth. Slowly he took his mother's hand and touched it to his lips, at the same time clicking his heels in a deferential bow.

"I trust you are well, Mother."

"Quite well, Carlos. We did not expect you back so soon."

"So I see. I am sorry to return at such an inopportune moment."

"It is not inopportune, my son, but you said you would be away until the end of summer."

"I was able to complete my business more quickly than I had anticipated." He glanced at his brother and then at Stephanie. "I see we have a visitor. A friend of yours, Miguel?"

"This is Miss North," Miguel replied. "She represents a firm of interior decorators from London. Mama has decided she can no longer live in draughts and damp. The Castelo is going to be completely redecorated."

"Not while I am the master," Carlos said sharply. "I will not have strangers wandering about my home! I thought I already made that quite clear."

"Please, Carlos." The Condesa's voice was thin and shaky. "Don't quarrel over it. I beg you to let Miss North stay and make a few improvements. It is so cold here in the winter – you know that for yourself – and I'm getting old. My bones are weak."

The man frowned and pulled at his lower lip. Nobody spoke and somewhere in the distance a clock chimed the half-hour. As the delicate silvery note died away he walked over to the sideboard and poured himself a drink.

"Very well, Mother. Miss North can do your apartment and that is all."

"How miserly of you, brother." Miguel's voice was full of irony. "Surely you will let her do the Long Gallery too? After all, the Collection must have a worthy setting."

Again antagonism flared and Stephanie sank further back in her chair, trembling at the dark fury on the Conde's face.

"One day you will try me too far, Miguel. I am warning you to be careful."

"You are the one that has to be careful." The young man's voice was arrogant. "I insist that the Long Gallery is done as well, and after that will come the library."

"Never!" The glass in Carlos's hand shook and liquid spilled to the floor. "While I am the master no one will touch the library. If they do it will be at their own risk!"

In bed that night Stephanie found it impossible to sleep, for her mind was uneasy with the strange surroundings, strange sounds, and the inexplicable behaviour of the master of the Castelo. What lay beneath the antagonism that brother had for brother, and why should the Condesa have sided with her younger son? For that was undoubtedly what had happened. The Conde de Maroc's journey abroad had afforded the Condesa and Miguel the ideal opportunity to repaint and refurbish the Castelo, and reviewing her explorations, Stephanie found it inexplicable that the present Conde had allowed his home to deteriorate so badly.

The atmosphere that evening had become strained and Stephanie had retired to her room as soon as she was able, leaving the family to sort the matter out between themselves. She had come to this job with high hopes and it was insupportable that the arrogance and bad temper of one man should now stand in her way. Not only would her father benefit financially by a job of this magnitude, but she herself had been given a chance to prove her mettle, and she was determined not to return to London without putting up some fight.

Resolutely she thumped the pillow and lay back in the feather bed. It was dark inside the room, for the moon seeped fitfully through the trees and the heavy furniture ranged against the walls loomed large in shadow form. Doors rattled on their hinges and timbers creaked as the wind howled round the turreted walls. Even in the height of summer, at such an altitude the nights were cold, and she huddled closer beneath the sheets and closed her eyes.

When she opened them again it was morning and bright yellow sunshine flooded the room. Hurriedly she washed and dressed and made her way downstairs, pausing in the hall as she wondered in which room breakfast was taken. Footsteps padded behind her and she turned to see Dinis, a tray in his hand.

"Breakfast is laid in the garden, *senhorita*, on the terrace beyond the drawing-room."

Slowly he padded ahead of her and she followed him out on to a large flagstoned terrace. Japanese maples and pink and blue hydrangeas sprouted in gaily tiled tubs and from the garden below came the cheerful chirping of birds and the rasping of cicadas. A bamboo table was set up at one end and silver platters heaped with croissants stood beside a steaming percolator.

"If there is anything else you require, *senhorita*, please ring the bell."

Without waiting for an answer the old man shuffled out of sight and Stephanie settled back to enjoy her breakfast and the scenery. What a far cry this was from London, with its dust and mist and teeming streets. With the turreted walls looming behind and the craggy mountain descending to the plains in front of her, it was easy to imagine herself in another era, where time had no meaning except as leisure to be whiled away.

With a sigh of content she began to eat, heaping her plate with cherry jam and pouring a cup of sweet, black coffee.

"If you'd rather have tea, Miss North, it can easily be arranged."

With a start that sent the liquid spilling, Stephanie looked up to see the Conde de Maroc in front of her.

"I'm sorry I startled you," he said.

She dabbed at the marks on her dress without replying and the man sat down and regarded her dispassionately.

"I must apologize for losing my temper last night. My only excuse is that I had a long journey and was tired."

"I'm sorry my presence was unwelcome." Still smarting from his behaviour of the night before, Stephanie was on her dignity. "You must appreciate, Conde, that I came here at the behest of your mother, not because I was touting for a job, as you seemed to infer."

He smiled. "I am sure you could never tout for anything. Now forget what I said and finish your breakfast."

Relenting, she sipped her coffee, studying him as he bent his head and took a cigarette from a thin, platinum case. He was as tall and dark as his brother but there the resemblance ended, for his features were square, his hair thicker and less controlled and his eyebrows so well marked they shadowed his eyes, making it difficult to define the expression that lay underneath. She guessed he was not a man to be intimidated or disobeyed, for command lay all over him like a cloak, showing in the thin mouth, the square chin and blunt hands, the little finger of which bore a heavy signet ring with the Maroc crest.

"You have a most unusual home," she remarked in the silence. "It must be one of the show-places of Portugal."

"It is." His tone was indifferent, with none of the pride she would have expected. "You are lucky to have seen it so intimately, Miss North. That privilege is given to very few strangers."

"I gather that. Is it because of the Collection?"

"Yes," he answered. "We have to be very careful."

"Where is it kept?"

"In an electrically wired room. We also have a dozen Alsatians in the grounds."

She shivered. "How unpleasant!"

"It is always unpleasant to be the custodian of wealth."

"Then why do you keep the Collection here?"

"Because I have not yet decided what to do with it. My father spent every waking hour examining the jewels, but to me they mean very little. I have always preferred flesh and blood to inanimate objects."

"You're not like your brother in that respect."

"I am not like my brother in any respect," he retorted, and lapsed into silence.

Stephanie stood up and walked over to the balustrade, leaning down to look at the gardens that sloped into the distance. A few men were tending the lawns and the shrubberies, and she heard deep-throated growls, which she supposed came from one of the Alsatian guards, though no dog was visible. Behind her she heard the Conde push his chair and his footsteps, slow and heavy, come across the flagstones.

"If you would care to see it. I will show you the Collection before you leave today."

"Leave?" She swung around. "What do you mean?"

"I thought I made that clear yesterday. It should not take you more than a few hours to decide what needs to be done to my mother's apartments. Then all you have to do is arrange for the work to be carried out."

"I'm afraid it's not as simple as that." Stephanie felt a familiar uprush of anger and determinedly kept her voice low. "When your mother wrote to my father – to the firm – she requested us to redecorate the whole of the Castelo. If you only want me to do one room I'm afraid the profit we make won't even cover my expenses in coming here. You must appreciate it's a long journey, Conde, and certainly not one that I would have undertaken just to redesign one room."

The man frowned and pulled at his lip. "I can see your point, Miss North, but naturally I will reimburse you for your time."

"That isn't the question at issue. I came here to do a job and I'll do it."

"You cannot."

"Why?" she persisted. "Believe me, I don't want to interfere in any private matters between you and your brother, but he's quite right when he says the Castelo is in bad need of attention. I found woodworm and a great deal of damp. If it isn't attended to right away it can be extremely dangerous."

Carlos de Maroc raised one thick eyebrow. "You seem very knowledgeable for such a small young lady."

Scarlet, Stephanie rounded on him. "My sex and my size have nothing to do with my brain!" She stopped and caught her lower lip between her teeth. "This job means a great deal to me, Conde. If I go home before it's finished my father will think I have failed."

"So!" the man said thoughtfully. "Does that mean you've had other failures?"

"Certainly not!" Furious that his assumption was so near the truth, her anger returned, and afraid that if she continued to speak she might say something she would regret, she turned her back and stared down at the lawn.

Behind her the Portuguese lit another cigarette, and as blue smoke drifted into the air he spoke again. "So you have found woodworm and damp in my home. I suppose you are sure of your facts, Miss North?"

"If you doubt my integrity, I suggest you call in somebody else."

"I do not doubt your integrity, Miss North, but I still think I'm at liberty to question people in my employ! However, as you are here, you might as well do what you came to do. But don't go near the library. That's one room I will not have touched!"

Not trusting herself to reply, she stepped past him and walked across the terrace and into the house, closing the door sharply behind her. Although the Conde's words could be interpreted as an apology, it was such a half-hearted one that Stephanie's anger was in no way appeased, and more than ever she wished she were free to leave.

She could not remember feeling so angry with anybody before as she did with this tall, self-assured man. Her instinct was to pack her things and leave the Castelo immediately, but the one thing that made her hesitate was the thought of having to confess another failure to her father after all her promises not to let him down. Yet she felt her position here was intolerable and for the moment she could see no way out of it.

Half-way up the stairs to her room she thought of Johnny

Carlton and stopped, wondering whether she should take him into her confidence. After a moment she turned and resolutely came down the stairs again, making her way across to the telephone. At least there could be no harm in asking his advice, and just to talk it over with a third person might help her to make up her mind.

She felt her spirits lift slightly at the sound of Johnny's cheerful voice at the other end of the line. "I need your advice," she told him. "Can I see you?"

"Of course," he answered at once. "I'll be right up and collect you and we'll go and have lunch together."

"That's fine. I'll start to walk down to Cintra to meet you."

Replacing the receiver, she ran upstairs for her jacket. As the door of the Castelo slammed behind her she breathed a sigh of relief and, humming softly under her breath, set out down the long drive in the direction of Cintra, pausing occasionally to examine a clump of flowers or look through a gap in the trees at the plain below.

The road wound continually and it was impossible to see farther ahead than a few yards. She wondered how long Johnny would be and hoped he would come to meet her before she reached the village. Again she paused, but although she listened she could hear no footsteps, and wiping the perspiration from her brow, she sat down on a boulder at the side of the road. It was a sultry day and as she rubbed her foot on the ground, grey dust rose in a cloud. Easing off her shoes, she rubbed one foot against the other. What a pleasure it was to relax, to get away from the uneasy atmosphere of the Castelo. Amazing how it had changed since the arrival of its master!

In the distance she saw the tall figure of a man, and afraid that it might be Carlos, she drew back into the shadow, only emerging as she recognized the fair hair and freckled face of Johnny Carlton.

She walked along the road to meet him, relief that it had not been the Conde making her greeting all the warmer.

"How nice to see you again! I can't tell you how pleased I was to hear your voice on the phone."

"Any English port in a storm, eh?" he grinned. "Not that I mind what your reasons were for ringing me as long as you did so." He touched her arm. "Don't let's stand talking in this heat. I've managed to hire an old jalopy – it's parked down the road."

Together they walked towards the ancient car drawn close into the hedge and Johnny held open the door for her.

"Not the height of comfort," he apologized, "but it's better than being in the sun."

He came round the side of the car and climbed in beside her. "Well now, how are you liking it at the Castelo?"

"It's an experience," she said cautiously.

"You sound as though it's also something of an ordeal." He studied her. "You look tired. What's the matter? Finding it a bit too tough?"

Warming to the sympathy in his voice, she launched into explanation, telling him of the Conde's unexpected return home and his strange behaviour when he had learned who she was.

"If I had any pride," she concluded, "I should have left the minute I learned his attitude. But this is such a wonderful commission for my father's firm that I don't want to let him down."

"I don't see why you should. You came up here at the Condesa's invitation and they've no right to go back on their word now."

"But it's unpleasant to stay if you know you're not wanted."

Johnny frowned. "I don't think you've any choice my dear. As you just said a minute ago, beggars can't be choosers, and right now that applies to you. If the Conde won't let you touch the library, you must pocket your pride and only do the rooms he wants you to. After all, it's not *your* business if he wants part of the Castelo left untouched."

Stephanie was silent, gazing thoughtfully out at the dusty landscape. Although she found Johnny's advice unpalatable, she knew that what he said was sensible.

"Very well," she sighed. "I'll stay."

"Good girl." His expression lightened. "That means I'll be able to see more of you. What time do you have to be back this afternoon?"

"As soon as we've had lunch. I've got a lot to do."

"Very well then. We'll go straight down to Cintra and have lunch at the inn and I'll drive you back again afterwards."

The village was filled with charabancs and tourists, all busy photographing the ancient palace that dominated the cobbled square and Johnny stopped the car outside the inn and led Stephanie to a table on the terrace.

"It's not the Ritz, I'm afraid," he said as they sat down, "but the food's excellent – providing you like Portuguese cooking!"

"I haven't had a chance to try it," Stephanie replied. "They have a French chef at the Castelo."

"That's just like the Conde – trust him to be different!"

Stephanie looked at Johnny curiously and wondered why he should have such a personal animosity to a man he had never met. It could not be the jealousy of a poorer man for a richer one, for Johnny was not that type of person, yet whenever he referred to Carlos de Maroc he did so with sarcasm.

Unaware of what she was thinking, Johnny picked up the menu and held it out. "You can order for yourself at your own peril."

She smiled. "I'd rather trust you – as long as you omit the garlic!"

"Impossible." Grinning, he studied the menu, gave his order to the waiter in a mixture of English and broken Portuguese and settled back in his chair.

"How's the book coming along?" Stephanie asked. "Any corpses in it yet?"

"Not one!" he grinned. "As a matter of fact it's not a

murder at all – it's about a jewel collection and I'm basing it on the Marocs."

"What a good idea!"

"I hope the rest of my public think so! I'm a great believer in making my stories as authentic as possible. And what I'd really like to do is to try and persuade your host to let me have a look at his collection. I thought you might be able to help me there."

"I'm not sure if I can. They're such a strange family that they might refuse. But I'll do my best."

"If not I'll have to use my imagination – plus your powers of description!" He filled her glass and set the wine bottle on the table.

She shook her head. "I haven't seen the Collection myself yet."

"Well, when you do, you can tell me all about it."

"Is there anything particular you'd like to know?"

The grey eyes shifted and gazed across the room. "Just if there are any unusual pieces of jewellery."

"What do you mean by unusual?"

He looked at her again. "Things like black pearls, or a collection of odd-shaped rubies. As a matter of fact, I'm particularly interested in unusual-shaped jewels. They're an important part of my plot." From his pocket he took out a newspaper clipping. "Here, take a look at this. It gave me the idea for the story in the first place."

Stephanie looked at the clipping. It was three months old and taken from an American newspaper.

"The Queen's Tear is the most unusual pearl of its kind in the world. One inch and three-quarters of an inch at the base, it is shaped in the form of a pear. It was first brought to public notice when purchased by Arturo Bordoza, the Brazilian millionaire, who added it to his collection five years ago. It changed hands a year later and was purchased by American heiress Mrs. Vandergeld, from whom it was stolen two months ago. All efforts to recover it have so far proved unsuccessful."

Stephanie handed back the newspaper cutting. "I don't see why anybody would want to steal a thing like that. You could never use it or break it up into smaller pearls to sell."

"I agree. But you can always find someone willing to buy it, simply for the joy of possession."

She looked at him inquiringly. "The joy of possession?"

"Yes. The person who has the Queen's Tear knows he can never put it on show. But he doesn't care so long as he can have the pleasure of gloating over it himself. You'd be surprised how many of these people exist – people who have a mania for beautiful things and don't care what evil they commit to get them."

She shivered. "You make it sound horrible!"

"It *is* horrible. You can't write books unless you know your subject and I've studied this one pretty thoroughly."

Stephanie moved in her chair and sighed. "Carlos de Maroc doesn't seem like a collector to me. Only a little while ago he said he wanted to sell everything."

"I wouldn't believe that. His father's been dead long enough for him to have sold out if he'd really wanted to. He's probably just covering up."

"Covering what up?"

Johnny Carlton shrugged. "It was just a figure of speech. You mustn't pounce on every word I say."

"I'm sorry." She crumbled a roll and determined to change the subject. "Let's talk about you for a change – something nice and personal like a fiancée or wife!"

"I'm not married." He grinned. "I like the free life too much."

"Do you think marriage and freedom incompatible?"

"Of course they are. You've only got to look at the married couples you know. They can never do a thing without consulting each other. No spur of the moment plans or decisions – which is the way *I* like to live."

"Unless you both have the same plans on the same spur of the moment."

"That's damn unlikely!"

She smiled. "I suppose so. Still, most people think it's worth sacrificing a certain amount of freedom to marry the person they love."

"I've never been in love, so I can't say."

"You'll feel the same when you meet the right person."

"Perhaps." He looked at her steadily. "In fact I might have met her already."

She coloured slightly. "If you had there wouldn't be any 'might' about it. You'd know."

"You sound as though you speak from experience!"

"I suppose a woman knows these things instinctively."

A plate of steaming food was put before her and with relief she picked up her fork and tasted it. "Very good. Top marks for Portuguese cooking so far!" She ate in silence for a moment and then reverted to their previous conversation. "Have you any family, Johnny? No parents or brothers or sisters?"

"Only my mother. My father died years ago and I'm an only child. How about you?"

She told him about her sister and parents and their house on the edge of Wimbledon Common.

"What about boy-friends?" he put in.

"Well, naturally," she laughed, "I'm not a hermit."

"I mean a special boy-friend?"

She hesitated. "No special boy-friend. Like you, I've never been in love."

"I find that hard to believe."

"Nevertheless, it's true."

Coffee and fruit were placed in front of them and she concentrated on peeling a peach. Sensing her reluctance to talk about her life, Johnny began to talk about some of the sight-seeing trips he had made, and then, as soon as they had finished eating, he paid the bill and led her out to the car.

Slowly they chugged up the incline, changing down as the road became steeper. Behind them they heard the high-powered whine of another car and Johnny drew into the side as a silver-grey Mercédès raced round the bend. Brakes screeched and a flurry of gravel was flung into the air as without slackening speed, it bowled down the drive towards the Castelo.

Johnny turned to her with a smile. "*He's* in a hurry! And it wasn't the chauffeur either. I take it, it must be one of the brothers?"

"It was Miguel."

"And the girl? You didn't mention there was another girl staying at the Castelo."

"There isn't. She must be a visitor."

Johnny whistled inelegantly. "Some visitor! I wouldn't mind meeting her on a moonlight night."

"I'll see what I can do for you!" Stephanie opened the door and jumped out on the road. "You needn't bother to take me any further. I'll walk the rest of the way."

Grey eyes smiled up at her. "I'll give you a ring one evening. Perhaps you'd let me take you into Lisbon?"

"Thanks," she said politely. "That would be very nice."

Walking along the drive Stephanie wondered whether her irritation with Johnny had anything to do with his obvious admiration for the dark-haired girl in the car with Miguel. Yet honesty forced her to admit that this was not so, for Johnny was not the sort of man to make her heart beat faster. Indeed, she had never yet met the man who could. Unwillingly the image of Carlos de Maroc flashed into her mind. Here was someone not to be trifled with: a man who knew his own mind and would not allow himself to be deterred from his course. She had seen him angry with his brother, tender towards the Condesa, and now she could not help wondering how he would behave towards the woman he loved. Arrogant, possessive, passionate: instinctively she knew he would be all three. To be loved by Carlos de Maroc a woman would have to give up her independence, but in so doing she might gain infinitely more.

There was no one visible when she reached the Castelo, but she caught a glimpse of hide luggage being carried up the stairs and knew that whoever the visitor was, she had come to stay for a considerable length of time. Closing the heavy oak door, Stephanie walked across the hall to the drawing-room. It was deserted and she went inside and looked around.

"This is the room I like the least."

She swung around to see Miguel. In flannels and a white sports shirt he looked more ordinary than usual, but there was still a certain cruelty about his mouth that dismayed her. She pushed the thought aside. Living at the Castelo de Arvores had made her fanciful. It would do her good to meet young feminine company. A few more weeks on her own and there was no knowing where her thoughts might lead her. She stepped back and looked round the room again.

"I don't know why you dislike it. I think it'll be very pleasant once it's redecorated."

"It will never be as beautiful as the library."

She sighed. "I agree. It seems a pity the Conde won't allow me to touch it."

Miguel tapped one finger-nail against the other. "I'll have to see what I can do. We really can't have the Castelo redecorated and leave the library untouched." He indicated a chair. "Sit down, Stephanie. I may call you Stephanie, mayn't I?"

"If you wish."

"Good. And you must call me Miguel." He smiled as she saw the colour rise in her cheeks. "Don't tell me you're shy! I didn't think English girls were."

"I'm not shy," she said coolly. "But I know Portuguese customs are different from ours."

"No matter," he said. "The attraction between a man and a woman is universal. It can bridge the gap between any country and any race."

There was a sudden sound of clapping and Stephanie turned swiftly as Carlos came across the room.

"I applaud that remark, Miguel," he said sarcastically. "It was spoken with such depth of feeling that it's a pity it happens to be completely untrue." The black eyes turned on Stephanie. "No doubt you agree with my brother, though?"

As always when confronted with the master of the Castelo, Stephanie's temper rose. "Why shouldn't I?"

"No reason at all. Women are incorrigibly romantic where sex is concerned." He moved to the fireplace and leaned his elbow against the mantelshelf. He too was wearing flannels and white shirt, but a dark blue muffler was knotted at his neck, its colour heightening his tan. "Unfortunately reality and romance are two different things," he continued. "No matter how much a man and a woman love each other there are always other considerations that cannot be overlooked, and this applies to everything in life. There's a right and a wrong, a good and an evil."

Miguel lit a cigarette and flicked the match into the grate. "And you, my dear brother, should certainly know the evil!"

Carlos did not reply but Stephanie saw the sudden colour that stained his cheeks, saw his narrow hands clench at his sides. Again she felt the antagonism between the two men and wondered what it was about Carlos that made Miguel take such pleasure in baiting him. Could it be jealousy that he was the head of the family or was it something deeper?

She moved over to the door. "If you'll excuse me I have work to do." Conscious of Carlos's sardonic expression she walked out, but was only half-way up the stairs when she heard him call her name and swung round to see him mounting the stairs towards her. Although he stopped two steps down from her, their eyes were almost level.

"When we parted earlier today you were very angry with me, Miss North. I hope you are feeling better disposed towards me now?"

Her colour heightened, but she did not answer.

"Well," he continued, "will you stay here under my conditions?"

"I have no choice."

"Good." His eyes narrowed. "Like most women you don't enjoy making an apology."

"I have nothing to apologize for," she said sharply. "And if one were due it would be more fitting if it came from you."

"Indeed!" His eyes glinted. "I did not know I had said anything to offend you. However, if I have . . ." His voice was low. "If I have then I do apologize – most humbly."

Watching him turn and walk down the stairs, Stephanie thought how ironical the last words were: most humbly! Anyone less humble than Carlos de Maroc she had yet to meet.

With the knowledge that there would be another guest present that evening, Stephanie dressed for dinner with particular care, and surveying herself in the mirror, knew there was a great deal to be said for her dark red hair and a slim figure. Her hair, held back from her face by two jewelled combs, fell in soft waves to her shoulders and her vivid green dress matched her eyes, the shimmering iridescent colour of a peacock's tail. The folds of chiffon billowed out behind her as she sped down the stairs, the glinting lights in the wall brackets outlining the delicate curve of arm and breast as she held her skirts high.

Below her the hall was in a pool of darkness and she did not see the man coming out of the library until she was almost on top of him. Too late she tried to stop, only saved from falling as Carlos put out his hands and caught her. Darker and more saturnine than ever in a dinner-jacket, he looked down at her, a long way down, until he found her eyes.

"Well, well," he remarked. "Where are you off to in such a hurry?"

She drew away from his arms. "I thought I was late for dinner. I'm sorry I nearly knocked you over."

"It would take more than a little thing like you to do that?"

She looked up at him. "I do wish you wouldn't keep calling me little."

"Very well." He bowed mockingly. "Come, Miss Giantess, let us go to the drawing-room."

Flushing angrily, she marched ahead of him and sat herself in a high-backed chair facing the fireplace, filled now with a bouquet of orchids instead of embers. The man walked over to a cabinet and came back with a large goblet. Stephanie took it from him and looked at the coating of sugar that frosted its rim.

Following her glance he smiled. "It's a champagne cocktail! The sugar improves the taste."

"I've never had one before," she admitted, and sipped. "It's delicious."

"I knew you'd like it." He sat down and tasted his own drink.

The silence between them was an uneasy one born out of awareness rather than indifference. It was apparent in the way the man avoided looking at her as she sat demurely in her chair, more apparent still when, drink in hand, he stood up and slowly roamed the room. After a few moments he came back and sat down again.

"How long do you think you'll be here?" he asked abruptly.

"A couple of weeks. I can assure you, Conde, that I'll get the job done as quickly as I can."

"I know you will. I am sure that like most English women you are quick and efficient."

She lifted her head. "Do you know much about English women?"

"Not very much. Only that they are of cold temperament."

Sudden anger made Stephanie speak sharply. "Why is it that the Latins always call English people cold? I've never heard anything so ridiculous!"

"I can assure you it's not ridiculous, Miss North. It happens to be true."

"I thought you said you didn't know us well enough to form an opinion."

"I've known enough English women," he said softly, "to know what they are like as lovers."

Their eyes met and there was an expression in his that made the blood run warm in her cheeeks. Her hand trembled and she set her glass down on the marquetry table beside her.

"In that case we'd better not continue this conversation, Conde."

"But I am enjoying it. Besides, I like to see you blush!"

Again she felt the tell-tale colour in her face and took up her glass to give herself something to do. Outside in the swift-falling dusk came the sonorous peals of a bell from a church in the village. Footsteps echoed on the stairs and the door was flung open.

A tall, slim girl with blue-black hair and a classic oval face came into the room and Stephanie recognized her as the girl in the Mercédès.

"Carlos darling!" The voice, light and well modulated, was as perfect as her appearance and equally as studied.

"Janique *cara*."

Carlos raised her hands to his lips and watching the man and woman, both so tall and dark, both so obviously of the same heritage, Stephanie knew a sudden sense of loss, as if something she wanted had been taken away from her.

"Carlos darling," the girl said again, "I hope I haven't kept you waiting."

"Knowing how long you take to dress, your arrival was as sudden as it was unexpected!"

Janique's lips parted in a smile that lost its warmth as she turned and saw Stephanie. "You must be the efficient Miss North I've heard so much about. I'm Janique Bonney."

Stephanie smiled back. "I didn't know my fame had gone ahead of me!"

"But of course." The girl sat down, the folds of her white dress falling back to disclose shapely ankles. "We're all terribly excited at the work you propose to carry out here. How long do you think it will be before it's all finished?"

"That depends on how quickly Portuguese builders work. I can only recommend what has to be done."

"I see. It's wonderful to meet a woman who's so business-like. I often wish I'd taken up something like that."

"It isn't as easy as it seems," Stephanie said drily.

"My dear, I'm sure it isn't. But I've a very good eye for colour, haven't I, Carlos?"

Carlos turned from the sideboard. "You certainly have. And good taste too: I like your dress."

"Thank you, darling. I hoped you would." She twisted round in her chair and looked at him. "I haven't seen your mother yet. She was resting when I arrived and I didn't want to disturb her."

"She has a bad headache and will not be coming down tonight. She asked me to give you her apologies and says perhaps you'll go up and see her before retiring."

"Of course, Carlos." She half stood up. "Shall I go now?"

"After dinner, my dear." His hand came out and rested on the slim shoulder, pushing her back into the chair.

Seeing the gesture, Stephanie felt suddenly in the way, and wished she were far from this elaborate room and these two exotic and alien people.

During dinner Janique, speaking mostly in Portuguese, monopolized the conversation, making no attempt to include Stephanie in it, and as soon as dessert was finished Stephanie asked to be excused.

"Will you not wait for coffee?" Carlos said indifferently.

"No, thank you. I want to start work early tomorrow and I have some things to get ready tonight."

She left the table and went to her room, knowing that her presence would not be missed. It was an unpleasant feeling, made more so by the fact that it was an unaccustomed one. At home she had always felt of some importance, but here she was a nonentity, an employee paid to do a job and depart as quickly as possible.

In her desire to complete the work at the Castelo, Stephanie concentrated harder than ever. She drew plans, made copious notes and compiled lists with feverish energy. It was not until one afternoon towards the end of the week that she threw down her pencil and rubbed her hands across her aching forehead. The pressure at which she had been working was beginning to tell and she knew that unless she took a few hours off, the throbbing at her temples would develop into a migraine that might incapacitate her for days.

Remembering the Condesa's offer that she could use the car, Stephanie told Dinis that she would like to go for a drive. "I won't be back for lunch," she said. "I'll have it in town."

The old man shook his head. "It is not fitting that you should go alone to a restaurant."

"Don't worry about me, Dinis. English girls always go out alone."

Leaving the old man still shaking his head, Stephanie went to her room to change and then hurried downstairs again. Her hair was tied back with a wide band of blue silk, the trailing ends of which fluttered in the breeze and her full skirt of the same material lifted slightly as she ran down the steps to the green Lagonda parked in the drive.

The chauffeur was at the wheel and she climbed in beside him.

"Where you like to go?" he asked in halting English.

"I haven't a clue," she grinned. "And I don't really care."

It was true she thought to herself, as she leaned back in her seat. The mere act of leaving the Castelo behind gave her a sense of freedom that she had not felt since she had first met Carlos de Maroc.

They drove swiftly along the dusty roads, hot and shimmering under the fierce sun, and Stephanie relaxed in the seat and tried to put Carlos, the Castelo and the whole Maroc family out of her thoughts. She wanted simply to be at peace and enjoy her short spell of relaxation. She knew that in her anxiety to get the job finished she had been driving herself too hard, and hoped that even a day away from her work would enable her to return to it with increased vigour.

Staring through the windows at the passing countryside, she was struck once again by the variety of colour in the Portuguese landscape, and also by the many different plants and trees that one would never have expected to see growing side by side: cacti raised their prickly fingers as though in an endeavour to reach the green, sticky-looking leaves of the palm trees; aloes and tree-ferns flourished amicably together and a forest of Portuguese cypress quickly gave way to maples.

The steady humming of the car and the gentle motion soon lulled her into a semi-doze and it was not until nearly an hour had passed that she roused herself sufficiently to ask the chauffeur where he was taking her.

"Estoril," he replied. "All people coming Portugal must go Estoril. Is very fine place."

"How far is it?" asked Stephanie.

"Are nearly there." The chauffeur pointed a finger. "Just over hill – we get there five, ten minutes."

As if to make sure of this, he pressed his foot on the accelerator and the car bounded forward. Within a few minutes they were driving through the town and Stephanie sat up and looked about her with interest. Wide, tree-lined streets were flanked by large glass-fronted cafés, and on the boulevards themselves people sat drinking pre-luncheon aperitifs and chatting gaily. Long, shining cars glided along the road, the sun glinting on their bonnets, and crowds of people walked briskly along the pavements or wandered aimlessly, stopping every now and then to gaze into shop windows. In spite of the noise and bustle there was an atmosphere of relaxation and lazy warmth about the place, as though everybody had but one aim: to enjoy themselves.

Stephanie turned and spoke to the chauffeur. "If you'll find somewhere to park I'll wander round by myself and come back to the car after lunch – say in a couple of hours."

"Very well, *senhorita*." The man hesitated. "Is not good for young lady to go alone in restaurant."

Stephanie smiled. "I'll be all right. I'm used to taking care of myself."

The chauffeur shrugged and raised his eyes heavenwards in silent comment on the mad English. But without further remark he drove to the centre of the town and parked the car in the square.

Leaving the Lagonda, Stephanie chose the shady side of

the road and began to walk slowly along the boulevard, glancing about her with interest and every now and then stopping to look at a cleverly arranged display of material, clothes or shoes in a shop window. However, deciding to be firm with herself she came to a small shop set back from the road and marking the beginning of an arcade. In the window, on an elegant silver stand, was a hat. By the very fact of its being the only object on display, it commanded attention, but on its own merits it was charming enough to catch the eye. Of honey-coloured straw with a small crown and large brim, a pale blue chiffon ribbon swathed round the bottom of the crown was the only break in its severity. Stephanie gazed at it entranced. In her mind's eye she pictured it on her shining auburn head and when she glanced down at her dress and saw it matched the blue of the ribbon she was lost.

When she came out of the shop a few minutes later, her blue head-scarf was in her handbag and the straw hat on her head. Her eyes, reflecting the colour of the trimming, sparkled as she walked jauntily along, conscious of admiring glances from the male passers-by.

Soon she began to feel thirsty and longed for a comfortable chair and a cool drink in the shady lounge of one of the hotels. She stopped outside a large, white-pillared building and, glancing up, saw the words "Palace Hotel" glittering above the porch. Somewhat hesitantly she entered the lobby and going into a comfortable, cool-looking lounge on her right, sank into an armchair. With some difficulty she made the waiter understand that she wanted a fruit drink with ice in it, and once this was placed before her, she relaxed in her chair, sipping gratefully and watching the comings and goings of other people.

Her drink finished, she rose, and crossing the foyer entered a large dining-room. On the threshold she hesitated, somewhat intimidated by the fact that the room was more crowded than she had expected. Women appeared to be very much in the minority and those who were present were all in the company of a man. It seemed to her that on her entrance everyone in the room looked up and stared, and blushing at finding herself the focus of so many eyes, her courage deserted her and she began to withdraw.

At that instant she felt a hand on her shoulder and turning swiftly, was amazed to find herself looking up into the dark, handsome face of Carlos de Maroc. There was a humorous glint in his eyes as he smiled down at her.

"Don't tell me the cool English miss is shy of entering a restaurant on her own?" he queried mockingly.

"Of course not! I – I simply changed my mind, that's all."

His expression softened and he touched her lightly on the arm. "I don't blame you, my dear. Women do not often enter a place like this on their own and it is not pleasant to be stared at. Come," he pressed her arm, "as it happens, I am lunching here and it would give me great pleasure if you would join me." Without waiting for her assent, he drew her into the room towards his table.

A waiter immediately sprang to her side, handed her into a chair, bustled around with silver and glass and presented her with a menu. Stephanie stared uncomprehendingly at the numerous dishes listed in Portuguese.

Carlos smiled. "If you will let me order for you . . ." he began, and she looked up gratefully, reminded in that moment of Johnny.

"Please do," she said. "I haven't a clue what to choose."

He spoke rapidly to the waiter, who nodded several times, grinned widely and departed.

Carlos leaned back in his chair and studied the girl opposite him. "You are looking extremely charming. I don't think I've ever seen you in a hat before! You should always wear one."

Stephanie coloured faintly and put one hand up to finger the brim. "I saw it in a shop window just now and couldn't resist it."

"I'm glad you didn't, it's delightful, English women usually dress so as to disguise the fact that they're women." She opened her mouth to protest, but he continued speaking. "You haven't told me yet what you're doing in Estoril."

"Taking French leave," she replied a shade defiantly.

"French leave?" He looked surprised. "What is that?"

"Going away without asking if you can do so. It's rather like playing truant." She half smiled. "I was feeling so washed out I felt I had to get away for a while, and as your mother very kindly told me I could use the car whenever I wanted to, I thought I'd give myself a day off and get away from the Castelo."

"You were perfectly right," Carlos assented. "I have thought many times lately you were looking tired. There is no point in driving yourself so hard. The Castelo will not run away from you."

"I've been working hard for one reason only," she said with asperity, "and I should have thought you'd know what it was without my telling you."

"I do not understand. Please don't talk in riddles."

She stared into his dark face and saw by his expression that he really did not know what she meant.

"Go on," he said quietly. "You can't make statements and then not explain them away."

She bit her lip and wished he were not always so tenacious in following a conversation through to the end. "It was because – because I thought you wanted to be rid of me," she explained. "I know that my presence at the Castelo is a source of irritation to you – you've made that perfectly plain more than once. That's why I've tried to get things done as quickly as I could. I don't like being in anybody's way."

"And you believed you were in mine?" He put out his hand and covered hers as it lay on the table. "You have a strange habit of always misunderstanding me, Stephanie," he said softly.

Never before had he spoken her name and a pulse beat nervously in her throat. Accustomed to the free-and-easy use of Christian names amongst her own set of friends, she had at first thought it strange to be addressed as Miss North by both Miguel and Carlos de Maroc. Even when she had been associated with people for business reasons they had very soon started to call her by her first name. Now, for the first time, she appreciated the more conventional attitude of the Portuguese, for by using her name so unexpectedly Carlos gave the moment an intimacy that was both unexpected and delightful.

"I hope you don't mind my using your name?" he interrupted her thoughts. "But for a long time now I have been thinking of you as Stephanie."

She moistened her lips. "I don't mind at all. In England everyone calls everybody else by their first names almost as soon as they meet."

"That is a habit I deplore. I only allow my personal friends and family to call me Carlos."

She did not answer and stared down at her plate.

"There is no food on it," he said, laughter in his voice. "Unless of course you are so hungry that you want to eat the china?"

She looked up and seeing his expression, could not help smiling.

"That's better," he said. "And just in case you are determined to go on misunderstanding me, maybe I'd better make it very clear that I want you to call me Carlos too."

"I – don't think I can."

"You'll have to, because I won't answer to any other name!"

As if the conversation were closed, he withdrew his hand from hers and straightened in his chair. "Now that we have disposed of all this nonsense, we must decide what to do with ourselves today. It's a piece of luck that I happen to be in Estoril and as we are both here I would like to show you the sights before driving you home."

"But I came in the Lagonda."

"Never mind about that. As soon as we've eaten we'll go and tell Manoel he need not wait."

Realizing the futility of arguing with him. Stephanie said no more and gave herself up to the pleasure of a first-class meal. After a leisurely coffee and liqueur they left the hotel and strolled towards the square where the car was parked. Carlos murmured a few words to the driver, who saluted, got back into his seat and rapidly drove away.

"Now then," Carlos said. "I've got you completely to myself and at my mercy!"

"I'm not afraid," Stephanie laughed, but the laughter died on her lips as she saw a flame of passion darken his eyes.

"One day I'll remind you of that," he said huskily, and putting his hand under her elbow, guided her over to the Mercédès.

For the rest of the afternoon he drove around Estoril, pointing out the gleaming hulk of the casino that lay surrounded by dark palms, and then along the coast where exiled kings lived in royal splendour, until they reached the fishing village of Cascais where time seemed to have stood still. The grey-blue Atlantic washed the golden sands as fishermen hauled in their nets and black-gowned women carried heavy baskets of market produce to the village square. The old houses huddled close together and the gleaming American cars that drove along the cobbled roadways seemed out of place.

"It's like another world," Stephanie remarked as they sauntered along the narrow walk overlooking the ocean. I can imagine it being like this fifty years ago."

"Two hundred years ago it was also the same," Carlos replied, "and two hundred years hence it will be the same too."

"Providing we aren't exploded to eternity."

"If we live with that thought in mind we will not live at all. You can't think of the future, Stephanie, you can only live for the present."

"But you don't! With a heritage like yours, you must surely think of the future in the same way as you think of the past."

"A heritage like mine." As he spoke his eyes darkened, the lines on either side of his mouth deepening until they seemed etched in bitterness. "I never think of the future, my dear, only the present – today, this moment. And because you are here to share it with me I never want to look farther."

She stared into his eyes and felt as if she were drowning in their depths. "We'd better be getting back to the car," she said breathlessly. "We don't want to arrive at the Castelo too late."

"One day I will not let you run away like this," he said quietly, so quietly that she pretended not to hear.

Lying back in the seat next to Carlos, Stephanie leaned her head against the cushion and gave a sigh of happiness. How peaceful it was bowling through the sunlit countryside by the side of this man who, in spite of everything, she had come to admire so much. She felt relaxed in his company, at peace with the world and content to let tomorrow take care of itself. She looked at Carlos's strong brown hands on the wheel and stole a glance at his stern profile. He was concentrating on the road ahead, his glossy black hair lifting slightly in the breeze that came through the car window. As though aware of her gaze, he turned his head towards her.

"Enjoying yourself?"

"I've had a lovely time."

"Good. I hope you will have many more enjoyable times while you are here."

He returned his attention to the road and neither of them spoke any more. All too soon for Stephanie they turned into the drive and came to a stop outside the Castelo. She slid out of the car and turned to him.

"Thank you for a lovely afternoon," she said, and was half-way up the steps when he called her back.

"You've forgotten something."

In the dusky light she could not see his face but there was something in his voice which held her transfixed. "Forgotten something?"

"Yes. When you thank me for a pleasant day you should use my name – Stephanie."

She coloured. "I'm sorry. Thank you for taking me sightseeing, Carlos." She still heard his gentle laugh as she ran up the stairs to her room.

Quickly she changed into a fresh dress, bathed her hot face in cold water and applied fresh make-up. Half an hour later she went downstairs to the drawing-room. The room appeared empty and she wandered over to the French windows and looked at the garden below. A blue haze robbed the sun of its harsh colour and softened the vivid green of the grass and the bright, almost tropical hues of the flowers. She sighed, not realizing she had done so until a voice spoke behind her.

"You seem to have the cares of the world on your shoulders, Stephanie. Is anything the matter?"

Startled, she swung around to see Carlos watching her. "I didn't hear you come in," she said.

"I've been here all the time. I was sitting in the wing chair so you didn't see me." He looked at her appraisingly. "You've changed very quickly."

"English girls don't trouble about clothes," she said, so tartly that he burst out laughing.

"I asked for that. I knew my remark at lunch-time had annoyed you. But *you* don't need to spend a lot of time on your dress – you are too beautiful."

"Thanks for the compliment."

"I mean it," he protested. "But I can see you don't believe me." This time he sighed, a mocking one that brought a smile to her lips.

Moving away from him, she seated herself in front of the fireplace and crossed her hands demurely in her lap. He remained watching her in silence, then, as she did not speak, walked over to the sideboard and lifted the decanter. Without asking what she would like, he poured a sherry and brought it over to her.

"I hope you will keep your promise not to work so hard in the future," he said abruptly.

"Now that I know my presence here does not annoy you, I can do as you ask."

"Good."

The word was lightly spoken, but looking up, she saw the intensity of his gaze and the flippant reply she had been about to make died in her throat. As always at one of his ambiguous remarks she felt at a disadvantage, not knowing whether he meant it or not. She was relieved by the arrival of Janique and Miguel and as soon as the other girl spoke, Stephanie knew that Janique was aware that she and Carlos had been out together during the afternoon.

"You are a most annoying man, Carlos darling." Janique's voice held an undercurrent of reproach. "We waited lunch for you until half past one."

"I intended to come back," Carlos said suavely, "but I met Miss North at the Palace in Estoril and we lunched together."

"We met by chance," Stephanie felt emboldened to explain. "Until I set foot in the hotel dining-room I hadn't realized what Dinis meant when he said Portuguese women don't go out unchaperoned. If I hadn't met Carlos I'd have turned tail and run!"

Janique raised an eyebrow and with a sense of discomfiture Stephanie knew she had noticed her use of Carlos's name.

"You mustn't take notice of the men in this country," Janique said blandly. "They are all wolves."

"Come, come," Miguel chided. "We are merely sheep pretending to be what we are not."

"You have *your* opinion," Janique said delicately, "and you must allow me to have mine." She turned as the door opened and the Condesa came in. With a smile of pleasure the girl ran over to her, curtseying as she kissed the lined cheek. "You are just in time to prevent an argument, madame. I say that the men in Portugal are wolves, but Miguel does not agree with me."

The Condesa smiled too, and leaning on Janique's arm, allowed herself to be seated in an armchair. Stephanie watched the little tableau in front of her and, embarrassed by Janique's kittenish gestures, turned her head away. As she did so she encountered Carlos's gaze. Nervously she put her hand to her face and seeing the defensive gesture, he smiled and came over to her.

"Can always tell when you are out of countenance," he said. "You change colour like a chameleon. One moment pink as a rose, the next pale as a lily."

"Most redheads change colour quickly," she said coolly.

"You are not most redheads," he whispered back. "You are a very special one."

With an effort she kept her expression composed but wished that he would save his compliments for someone else. How difficult it was to assess a man like Carlos de Maroc. This afternoon he had been charm personified, an attentive host, a gracious and charming escort. He had spared no trouble to amuse her and to show her the sights of Estorial and Cascais. Indeed, she knew the hours she had spent in his company would be treasured like a jewel, brought out to remember when she returned to England. Yet underneath the charm there was a man of steel. Which was the real Carlos? It was a difficult question to answer, almost an impossible one. She moved back in her chair and as if sensing her withdrawal, he sauntered away.

Almost immediately Dinis came in to announce dinner and taking Janique by the arm, Carlos led her out. The Condesa and Miguel followed behind and Stephanie, alone as usual, brought up the rear.

At the dining-room door the Condesa stopped. "My handkerchief," she said. "I've dropped it."

Stephanie ran back to pick up the scrap of lace from the carpet, and as she recrossed the hall the old lady moved towards her.

"You are an obliging child," she said in her thin, emotionless voice. "If you will give me your arm?"

Slowly they moved into the dining-room. The table, set with elaborate silver and glass, was lighted by tall-stemmed candles that shed their white and waxy glow over a drift of roses that formed the centrepiece. Miguel had taken his seat at one end of the table and Carlos was holding a chair for Janique. As she slid into her place the girl turned her limpid eyes up to the man and an intimate glance was exchanged between them. Stephanie heard the old lady at her side give a faint sigh.

"What a lovely picture they make," she murmured half to herself. "If all goes well I hope they will announce their betrothal before the month is out."

Stephanie's hands trembled, and afraid that the Condesa might notice, she hurriedly took her own place at the table. So that was the reason for the lovely girl's visit to the Castelo! It was the obvious choice for Carlos to want a woman of his own race, a woman who would be a suitable chatelaine for his home.

Stephanie picked up her fork and began to eat, but the food was tasteless and the wine, red as rubies in the crystal glass, might as easily have been water.

CHAPTER FOUR

STEPHANIE spent a restless night: each time she was on the point of sleeping, pictures of Carlos and Janique, vivid as though they were there in person, flashed across her mind and jerked her into wakefulness. Carlos and Janique: both so handsome and vibrant, so ideally suited to each other. But why should thoughts of them torment her and disturb her rest? Neither of them was her concern. Portugal didn't suit her, she decided: it was making her fanciful and restless, and the sooner she returned home the better.

With this thought uppermost in her mind she went to work early the following morning in the upstairs *salon*. Once again she was entranced by the beauty around her. This part of the Castelo was the best preserved, the gold paint on the carved walls still bright, the murals either side of the marble fireplace still depicting clearly scenes from the surrounding countryside. At one end of the room double doors led to the gallery where the Maroc Collection was housed. It had not been opened since her arrival and occasionally she glanced towards it, wondering what lay beyond. Absorbed in her work she did not hear anyone approach, but some sixth sense made her aware that she was being watched. Turning, she saw Carlos framed in the doorway, a cigarette in one hand, the other in the pocket of his corduroy jacket.

She scrambled to her feet, pushing her hair out of her eyes. "Good morning, Conde. Did you want to see me?"

"Not specifically. I was looking for Janique – Dinis told me she came up here."

"I haven't seen her – and I've been here since nine o'clock."

He glanced at the pad in her hand. "What remains to be done when you have finished making notes?"

"I suggest you call in another consultant to help you choose your colour scheme."

He stared at her in surprise. "Isn't colour a part of interior decorating?"

She bit her lip. "Yes, of course. But I thought it might be better for somebody else to do it for you."

"Rubbish," he interrupted. "As you are here you must do the whole thing. Besides, I don't like having strangers underfoot."

"Is that the only reason?" she retorted and, as she saw his smile, regretted her remark.

"Of course it's not the only reason," he said softly. "Are you fishing for compliments so early in the morning?"

"I never fish for compliments."

"Good. Then I will not bother to give you any." His smile widened. "A pity you have such bright red hair, Stephanie – if it were not for that, you would practically melt into your surroundings."

Inexplicably her spirits rose, and forgetting the sleepless hours she had spent, she smiled at him. "Are you willing to leave the colour scheme to me?"

"Of course. Providing you stick to pastels: delicate pinks and blues with an occasional touch of green."

At his precise instructions she burst out laughing. "In other words any colour as long as it's the one *you* want!"

"Exactly. Go into Lisbon and have a look around the shops. There are many good ones. It's not Paris, you understand, but you will none the less find plenty to choose from. At the same time you can also meet the Portuguese firm who will be your sub-contractors. I suggest Alfonso Lajos, they are excellent."

Although realizing that Carlos would know the best builders to approach, Stephanie could not help the irritation that welled up in her at his taking the decision out of her hands. However, her short acquaintance with him had taught her not to argue: that would only make him more adamant. Far better to give in gracefully than be forced to submit to his will.

"I'll go and see whoever you suggest," she said demurely. "Then if they're no good you'll only have yourself to blame!"

The thin mouth parted in a smile, but whatever remark he might have made remained unsaid, for at that moment Janique strolled into the room.

Today the French girl was resplendent in strawberry silk, a colour that enhanced the dusky bloom of her skin and the liquid dark eyes that looked at Carlos with an expression of beguiling innocence.

"What a naughty man you are, *amado*. I thought you'd run out on me!"

"On the contrary, I've been looking for you. I thought we might go for a drive."

"What a wonderful idea!" Janique linked her arm in his. "I'd like to get a few things in Lisbon."

Carlos raised an eyebrow. "If we're going to Lisbon, we can give Stephanie a lift."

Janique looked so disconcerted that Stephanie hid a smile.

"You needn't bother," she said quickly. "I'm not sure what time I'll be free to go in."

"It's no bother," Carlos said abruptly. "We'll be leaving in half an hour. See that you are ready."

Giving Janique his arm, he walked out, leaving Stephanie to stare after him in exasperation.

Sitting in the back seat of the Mercédès-Benz later in the morning, she thought how typical the offer was of the man; a kind gesture cloaked by rudeness: no matter how one looked at it, it was more comfortable to journey in a car than in the small electric train that travelled the coast to Lisbon.

Within a short time they approached the city: the narrow roads gave way to wide avenues and tree-lined boulevards, on either side of which stood cream stone houses with narrow windows marked by wrought-iron grilles. They crossed the main square and drove down the Avenida da Liberdade.

Unlike the main roads of most of the capital cities, there were a few fashion shops lining the *avenida*, and for the most part the windows displayed ironmongery and other mechanical goods designed to appeal to men. At the end of the avenue Carlos drew the car to a stop.

"That steep road directly in front of you is the Rua Augusta," he said. "There you will find everything you want."

"Thanks." Stephanie clambered out of the car, aware as she did so of Janique's insolent look. "It was kind of you to drive me in."

"Not at all. How long do you think you'll be?"

"I don't know. A couple of hours maybe. Anyway, I'd like to stay in Lisbon this evening and have a look round."

"Of course." He leaned his head out of the window. "I'm forgetting you're really a tourist. Meet me at the Avis Hotel at seven o'clock tonight and I'll show you something not many tourists see." He turned to Janique. "Will it suit you if we don't get back to the Castelo till late?"

As he spoke to Janique, Stephanie knew a moment of desolation so sharp that it seemed to take physical form. She shivered and shook the feeling off, knowing she had no right to command his sole attention.

"Well, Janique," he said again. "I want to take Miss North sightseeing tonight. If you'd rather not come I'll drive you back to the Castelo."

"Don't be silly, darling," the girl answered. "I came all this way to be with you and I'm not going to let you out alone – particularly with a pretty, unchaperoned girl."

Stephanie felt herself colour, growing even pinker as Carlos fixed his dark eyes on her.

"Keep out of the sun," he said matter-of-factly. "It will not suit you to freckle."

Biting her lip to hide her mortification, she turned away from the car and began to walk up the steep street ahead. As Carlos had rightly said, the Rua Augusta was lined with shops, each one trying to out-do the other. Handbags and jewellery, shoes, perfume, all were displayed with lavish abundance, while bales of delicate materials with metallic threads of gold or silver running through them were heaped in piles in the windows of the main store. Reluctantly deciding that she must get patterns before sampling any of the Portuguese wares, Stephanie took out her notebook and methodically began to work through each room. Samples of brocade were chosen for chairs and curtains, snippets of wool were procured for rugs, and armed with these samples she hailed a taxi and rattled along the streets to the imposing marble façade of the building firm suggested to her by Carlos.

The interior office of Alfonso Lajos was less impressive than the outside, for here were the same utilitarian desks common to most offices, the same busy typists and men hurrying backwards and forwards with files tucked under their arms.

The name of Maroc worked like magic and within a moment of uttering it Stephanie was presented to Senhor Lajos himself. Carefully she outlined the work she had done at the Castelo, and speaking on her father's behalf, formally engaged the Portuguese to carry out the necessary reconstruction.

"The Condesa called my father's firm in," she continued, "and it's the first time we've taken on a commitment outside England."

"If you are successful with this job – as I am sure you will be," Senhor Lajos said grandiloquently, "many more commissions will follow. The Maroc family are of international fame. You have heard of the Maroc Collection, no doubt?"

"Yes," Stephanie replied, "I have."

"Then you will appreciate what an honour it is for me to work for the family. I will personally supervise the job." He thumbed through the specifications Stephanie had placed before him, his full lips pursing in a smile as he read the closely written sheets. "You have itemized everything," he said at last. "From what I can see there will be no need for you to stay on. I will communicate direct with your firm should any difficulty arise."

Stephanie pushed back her chair and stood up. "I didn't intend to stay on anyway. I've spent long enough in Portugal."

"You speak as if you don't like it."

"I like it very much," she replied, and it was only as she left Senhor Lajos behind that she wondered whether she had not grown to like it too much.

Portugal was a country that crept up on one; insidiously, gently, one was engulfed by its beauty and its magic. Poverty went hand in hand with riches, colour with drabness. It was a land forever changing, yet in some strange way remained as it had been centuries ago when Columbus had set out to discover the new world.

How easy it would be to stay on at the Castelo, to allow herself the luxury of a few more weeks. Weeks with whom? It was a question she was loath to answer, and she hurried along the road, wishing she were able to leave for London at this very moment.

The Avis Hotel slumbered amidst dark green foliage, resembling a mansion of shabby splendour rather than a hotel of international repute. The lounge was discreetly quiet, as was the conversation of the few people who inhabited it. Janique and Carlos were sitting at a corner table, the French girl looking so elegant in her slim dress that Stephanie wished she were wearing something less serviceable than a tailored linen suit. She walked towards them, her heart thumping as Carlos stood up and came across to meet her.

"So you did come!" he said softly.

"Of course. I promised."

"Was it only your promise that brought you here? You've no idea how rebellious you looked when I suggested it."

Without replying she preceded him to the table and, determined to keep their meeting on a business level, launched into a detailed account of all she had done that afternoon. Carlos listened attentively, not saying anything until she told him of her meeting with Senhor Lajos.

"I think my father will be pleased with him," she concluded, "particularly as I engaged him on your recommendation!"

The dark eyes flashed. "How diplomatic you are!"

Janique stirred in her chair. "Did you buy anything for yourself, Miss North? Or were you too busy?"

Glad to change the conversation Stephanie grinned. "No woman is too busy to shop – particularly when she's abroad: I'm afraid I did succumb to the lure of the shops. As a matter of fact I bought a pair of shoes. I'm wearing them now and they're sending my others back to the Castelo."

She lifted her foot and looked at the scarlet pump.

"Very nice," Carlos said. "You have beautiful legs."

Her face the same colour as her shoes, Stephanie hastily pulled down her skirt and Janique, her smile controlled, leaned forward to take a cigarette from the package on the table.

"Personally, I think there's nothing more boring than going out with a tourist. They exclaim over everything and have no sense of discrimination. Everything is either wonderful or terrible."

"Surely discrimination only comes with travel?" Stephanie replied. "And not everyone can afford to do that. This is *my* first trip," she added pointedly.

"Then you are to be excused. I have been abroad ever since I was a child. My mother is Portuguese, but my father is French, and he was a Consul for many years."

"Janique is one of the most travelled young ladies you're likely to meet." Carlos's voice was expressionless. "Sometimes I wonder that she stays so long in Portugal."

"Now you're fishing for a compliment," Janique said lightly, "and I'm not going to give it to you, *amado*."

Stephanie leaned back in her chair as if by so doing she could withdraw from the conversation, and noticing the movement Carlos got to his feet.

"It's time we were leaving. I'm going to take you to a little restaurant for dinner where you can hear the *fados*."

Curiosity dispelled Stephanie's embarrassment. "Aren't those Portuguese folk songs?"

He nodded. "They are usually morbid and often monotonous. But it is the one thing that a Portuguese away from home always longs to hear. One of our writers once said that the *fados*, the knife and the guitar are the three things adored by the people of Lisbon."

"How primitive," Stephanie shuddered.

"But we are!" he said quietly. "You will do well to remember that."

Sudden dusk had settled on the city as they drove into the poorer quarter. It was as if they were entering another country, another age. Narrow alleyways, dark and smelling of spices and wine and filth, wound steeply in all directions, so tortuous that it was impossible to drive through them. Carlos parked the car and, taking Janique and Stephanie by either arm, guided them along the road.

"It's only a little way," he apologized. "Not worthwhile getting a taxi."

"I'd much rather walk," Stephanie said. "You never get the feel of the city if you ride."

"And that is important to you?" He leaned forward until his dark face was so near to her own that she could have put up her hand and touched it. The warm wind of Lisbon rustled the dust at their feet and she stepped back, catching her breath on a sigh.

"It's always important for me to know – everything."

Instantly there was a shuttered look on his face. "You are like most women. Curious, imaginative, never leaving well alone."

It was a strange remark and Stephanie pondered over it as they climbed a steep hill, traversed a road and walked down another dark alley to a small restaurant. Gaily coloured cloths chequered the tables and candles spluttered golden light across the whitewashed walls and timbered ceiling. The heavy smell of garlic and paprika hung in the air and in one corner a guitarist and pianist were playing. Carlos guided them to a table and spoke in rapid Portuguese to the proprietress, who waddled over to them. There was much "*si-si-ing*" and many gesticulations before she finally bowed herself away and Carlos leaned back in his chair and smiled.

"I have taken the liberty of ordering for both of you. Your taste I know, Janique. Miss North's I shall have to guess."

"That shouldn't be difficult," Janique remarked. "Miss North is a typical product of her country. An English flower – frank and open!"

Stephanie wondered whether she were unduly sensitive, for the words, instead of sounding complimentary, seemed by some subtle intonation to become an insult. Many answers came to her mind, but all of them would have provoked a further retort, and deciding diplomacy was called for, she said nothing, relieved when the waiter set plates before them. The meal Carlos had ordered was typically Portuguese. It began with small pieces of fish floating in a thick stew, the whole flavoured with spices and onion; then wafer-thin escalope of veal braised in cream, washed down by a slightly bitter red wine.

They were sipping coffee when the pianist strummed a chord, the guitarist came forward to the centre of the room and the fat proprietress untied her apron, moved to stand beside him and started to sing. Instantly the crowd became silent, the only movement in the room being the hands of the two musicians and the writhing trails of blue cigarette smoke. The woman's voice had a husky tone, the vibrant quality only possessed by an untrained voice. Starting slowly, almost monotonously, she soon became overwhelmed by the sadness of her song and her voice rose higher as she swung her body from side to side. Faster and faster the pianist played, louder and louder strummed the guitar, until the whole room was filled with the heavy throbbing beat of music so primitive that it attacked the senses. With a suddenness that was startling the song ended and the woman seemed to wake from her trance to accept the hysterical acclamation of the audience.

Stephanie sat back exhausted, for although she had not understood the words, she was moved by the pathos that underlay them. Looking up, she saw Carlos watching her. He moved his head and his dark eyes glittered, staring at her as if they could probe the very secrets of her heart. She shivered and surreptitiously wiped her trembling hands on her serviette.

With an abrupt gesture he pushed back his chair and stood up. "We must return to the Castelo. I'm expecting a telephone call from America at ten o'clock."

Janique made a face. "Can't we stay a little longer? I'm sure Miguel could take the call for you."

"That is out of the question." Carlos's voice was grim enough to brook no further argument, and with another shrug Janique stood up.

Once more in the car, Stephanie looked out at the flat landscape. The drab fields, many of them barren and swept by wind and sand from the seashore, were now silvered in moonlight, giving them a radiance they did not possess in the harsh light of day. Carlos drove fast, not even slackening speed as they sped through the village square of Cintra and up the steep mountain road that led to the Castelo. Round the hairpin bends they went, the car swinging so precariously that Stephanie's mouth grew dry. With a further burst of speed they passed through the gates and along the drive, drawing up with a screech of brakes at the front door.

Together they entered the vast hall and Janique smoothed down the folds of her dress and lifted her heavily lidded eyes to Stephanie. "You must be tired," she drawled. "If you'd like to go to bed I will see that one of the servants brings you up a hot drink."

Stephanie glanced at Carlos, but his face was devoid of expression and instinctively she knew he was impatient to be alone. With a murmured "goodnight" she went upstairs, and in the seclusion of her bedroom pushed wide her window and laid her elbows on the sill, the mountain air damp against her skin. From this elevation her eyes stretched over the country with its deep wooded slopes, and in the far distance, obscured now by night, the shifting, glimmering sea. Directly below her lay the terrace and beyond that the garden. A light glowed and she leaned out to watch it. Hidden by the trees, it suddenly glowed again and she wondered if it were the tip of a cigarette. Yet it cast too large an area of light along the avenue of trees, and with a shiver of fear knew that somebody was outside: an intruder perhaps, or a servant?

Then, in the still air laughter trembled and a light voice spoke in the lilting cadence of Portuguese. Recognizing Janique's voice, Stephanie drew back into her room. No doubt she and Carlos were taking a stroll in the grounds.

Slowly she started to undress, but it seemed too early to go to bed and, slipping on a pair of flat-heeled shoes and a woolly cardigan, she decided to take a walk in the garden. The night air might do her good, help to relax her tautened nerves. Quietly she crept downstairs and skirting the side of the house, walked lightly over the lawn towards the small rose arbour which lay some hundred yards from the Castelo. She was half-way down the steps that led to the sunken garden before she realized it was occupied. Carlos and Janique were standing by a small goldfish pool and as she watched, the French girl placed her hand on Carlos's shoulder. Moonlight shone full on Janique's face, disclosing the line of brow and chin and the graceful column of her neck. She murmured something, for the red lips moved gently, stretching into a smile as Carlos bent his head and drew her into his arms. With a sudden abandon entirely unlike her usual carefully planned movements, Janique twined her arms round the dark head and, watching the slim white fingers caress the black hair, Stephanie knew an intense moment of anguish. Hardly aware of what she did, she stepped back into a cluster of bushes, not caring where she went as long as she could obliterate the two figures so close together.

On and on she stumbled, disregarding the briars that pulled at her skirt and the overhanging branches of the trees that brushed against her hair. When she finally stopped walking she was in a part of the garden she had never seen before. Towering bushes masked the way ahead while to the left a rushing torrent of water cascaded down a bank in a miniature waterfall. Panting, she rested against the trunk of a tree and closed her eyes. A twig snapped and she tensed, instinctively aware that she was not alone. She opened her eyes and looked round her, but the shadows loomed dark and the sliver of moon, half hidden by clouds, only served to emphasize the blackness. Again there was the sound of a stealthy pad, and with fast-beating heart she remembered the pale patch of light she had seen from her bedroom window a few moments ago. Nervously she moved away from the tree and as the sound came again she remembered the priceless Maroc Collection and the savage dogs that were supposed to roam the garden. In sudden panic she turned and ran back along the path. Footsteps sounded behind her, increasing their pace to match hers. The distance between them shortened and desperately she plunged into the cover of some bushes. Arms came round her and she screamed, fighting them with all her strength.

"Let me go! Let me go!"

But the arms did not relax their hold and one hand came up to her mouth. "Be quiet," a voice whispered. "For heaven's sake be quiet."

Stephanie relaxed so suddenly that she almost fell. "Johnny!" she gasped. "Was it *you* I've been running away from?"

"Of course it was me."

Letting her go, Johnny stepped so that she could see his face. In a dark suit it was not surprising he had been almost invisible in the garden and Stephanie's curiosity stirred as she saw he was also wearing gloves and carrying a torch.

"What are you doing here?" she asked suspiciously. "Getting more local colour?"

"Well, no. As a matter of fact I . . ." He tensed and before she knew what was happening, caught her into his arms again and pressed his mouth on hers. It was impossible to struggle: tall and thin though he was, his muscles seemed made of steel and gripped her so fiercely that it was painful to move.

"I'm sorry to break up the tête-à-tête," a low voice said behind them, and Johnny's hands dropped away from Stephanie, enabling her to step back and look with dismay into the sardonic face of Carlos de Maroc.

"I thought I heard voices," he said coldly. "How did you get in here?"

Johnny moved forward. "I climbed over the wall – narrowly missing the electrified wire at the top, I might say."

"You were fortunate," Carlos said even more coldly. "You'd have been a corpse by now had you touched it."

"I was careful of that," Johnny said easily. "But I couldn't resist my rendezvous with Stephanie." He caught her hand in his, the pressure of his fingers on her palm warning her to silence. "We arranged to meet down here because I understand you don't care for visitors at the Castelo."

Carlos turned and looked at Stephanie. "Is this true? Did you arrange to meet this man here?"

Stephanie looked into the dark eyes and the expression of mockery she saw emboldened her to a defiance she did not feel.

"I certainly did," she replied. "Mr. Carlton is a friend of mine. I take it you've no objection to my meeting a friend – even if it is on your property?"

"More than a *friend*," Carlos answered, "judging from the little scene I interrupted."

"You know how it is, old boy," Johnny said cheerfully. "These tropical nights are made for love."

"No doubt." Carlos lit a cigarette, the flicker of light showing the thin line of his mouth pulled down at the corners with anger. "I'd still be obliged if you'd clear out of these grounds and in future arrange to meet Miss North in a less secretive way."

Without another word he strode down the path and as his figure disappeared Stephanie pulled her hand away from Johnny.

"I won't have you implicating me in something I don't understand. Why on earth did you tell him you came here to meet me?"

"I had no choice. My saying that scotched his suspicions. He'd have wondered what I was doing otherwise."

"He certainly would. And so am I. What are you up to? You behaved oddly from the first moment we met."

"I told you. I'm writing a book and I want local colour."

"That's still no reason for you to sneak in here like a – like a thief."

The moment the words were out a horrifying suspicion entered her mind. The colour receded from her cheeks and she knew that Johnny was instantly aware of it. His hand gripped her by the shoulder and pulled her into the cover of the bushes.

"If you don't let me go," she said furiously, "I'll scream! I should have guessed what you were up to from the minute—"

"Be quiet!" he said. "You'll ruin everything if you aren't quiet."

"I intend to ruin everything if you're after the Maroc Collection!"

Her voice rose and his hands came over her mouth. "*Please!* You've got it all wrong. The last thing I am is a thief." He bent nearer. "I can see the only way to shut you up is to tell you the truth, but you've got to give me your word you'll keep mum."

Stephanie raised her head and looked into the light grey eyes so near her own. "Who are you?" she said faintly. "What are you trying to do?"

Johnny relaxed his hold and, stepping back, stared at her

for a long moment without answering. "I'm a detective," he said at last. "And I'm looking for stolen jewellery."

"But why *here?*"

"Because," he said slowly, "I've good reason to believe this is where I'll find it."

CHAPTER FIVE

WISPY grey clouds scudded across the sky, disclosing the face of the moon, and in the hard silver light Stephanie stared at Johnny in horror.

"I can't believe it!" she gasped. "A detective? But what do you hope to find here? The Maroc Collection belongs to the family."

"It's not the Maroc Collection I'm interested in. It's other jewellery, equally valuable but belonging to other collections." He caught her hand and drew her into the darkness of the bushes. "I know this must be a shock to you, but now I've told part of the truth, I might as well tell you the rest of it."

Keeping his voice low and occasionally stopping to make sure that no one was approaching, Johnny explained that he was employed by a group of insurance companies as their private investigator, his job to trace jewellery which had been stolen over the past few years from different countries. None of it had found its way on to the regular market, neither was there any evidence that it had been broken down into smaller pieces and sold. That left only one possibility: the jewels had been bought by someone who wanted them for their beauty alone.

"Those sort of people are the most difficult to track down," Johnny went on. "They hoard the things like misers and when they die, take the secret with them to the grave. These private collections have a habit of passing from one person to another without anyone ever being the wiser."

"It seems very far-fetched to me," Stephanie retorted.

"Far-fetched or not, it's the truth. Don't you remember the newspaper cutting I showed you a couple of weeks ago? The Queen's Tear? That will never be found again, mark my words. A pearl like that can never be resold or worn openly."

"What's that got to do with the Marocs?"

"Nothing, probably. I'm just trying to give you a picture of the set-up I'm fighting."

A thin breeze stirred the leaves and the moon was again obscured by cloud. In spite of Johnny's answer Stephanie felt a tremor of fear go through her and it was a moment before she spoke again. "Why are you so interested in the Marocs?" she asked.

"Because every clue I've followed since I've been working on this case has led me here. I'm almost sure Carlos de Maroc is the man I'm looking for."

"I don't believe it!" The words were forced from her and she only realized how vehement she sounded as she saw the look on Johnny's face. Instantly she tried to cover up. "I mean he – he seems so honourable – I'm sure you're wrong."

"Then why is he so careful about intruders? What has he got to hide?"

"With the Collection in the Castelo you wouldn't expect him to leave all the doors open, would you?"

"There's more in it than that," Johnny muttered. "I'd give my right arm to be let free in that place."

"Well, don't look at me," she said hastily. "I've done enough lying for you tonight."

The Englishman took out a cigarette, and looking at his expression in the glow of the match, she wondered how she could ever have thought him easy-going, for his face was set and pale, the mouth a thin line of determination that added years to his age.

"I'd better be going back, Johnny. I'm tired."

"Don't go yet. I'd like to talk to you."

"Can't it wait till tomorrow?"

"You might give me the brush-off then!" He put his hand on her arm. "Look, Stephanie, this job means a great deal to me. If I can crack this case it'll lead to promotion, but more than that, it'll put an end to a filthy racket."

"What do you think I can do?"

"A great deal if you're willing."

"I'm not going to be your spy!"

"I only want you to keep your eyes and ears open. You can't live in a place day after day and not pick up something."

"Johnny, no!" She pulled away from him. "You'd have had to manage if you'd never met me. Why can't you forget you ever did?"

"Now you're talking like a child." He came closer. "Why should it matter to you whether the Marocs are guilty or not?"

His question caught her by surprise and she was triumphant at the answer that came swiftly to her lips. "Because I'm employed by them and owe them some loyalty. Besides, this job means a great deal to my father and I want to get it completed."

"And I want to get mine completed too. For God's sake, Stephanie, if somebody from Scotland Yard asked you to help them you wouldn't refuse. Why can't you look on my request as the same sort of thing? The police in Lisbon know who I am. They can vouch for me."

Suddenly she was tired of arguing. Words could be bandied between them for ever and yet still not disclose the real reason for her reluctance to help him. It stemmed, she knew, from a desire to protect Carlos, although why she should want to protect someone who gave every indication of being able to look after himself, she did not know. Yet Johnny too deserved her help. Like herself he was English, like herself he was fighting to prove that he was capable of keeping his job. If she promised to help him she would be doing no more than any other English girl would do in the same circumstances.

"All right," she said quietly. "I'll keep a watch out for you. But I'm sure you're wrong."

He smiled. "We won't argue about that. Thank you, Stephanie. I don't think I'd better be seen around the Castelo for the next few nights. If you've anything to tell me you can get me at the inn. I'll be there most nights."

"All right." She turned away, but he caught her shoulder

and twisted her round. "I must have a goodnight kiss," he whispered against her hair. "The Conde would think it peculiar if I didn't!"

Before she could stop him he pressed his mouth on hers and then stepped back, waving with every appearance of the young lover as she sped out of sight.

Alone in her room Stephanie found it impossible to sleep. Everything Johnny had told her came back to torment the night hours, and listening to the wind stir the branches of the trees and the leaves rustling on the terrace below, she found it difficult to push aside the doubts that filtered into her mind as she remembered the many times Carlos had absented himself from his home during the last few years. "He's always travelling abroad," Miguel had said. "He's more away from home than in it." Yet all his ties were here: why should he find it necessary to travel? "Perhaps he likes travelling," she argued with herself. "He's rich enough to go where he likes. Why should he stay in Portugal all the time?"

Gradually the sky changed colour, waning from midnight blue to grey, tinged with the pink of the rising sun. She threw back the bedclothes, and heavy-eyed from lack of sleep, started to dress. She could not spy on Carlos, that much was certain. As long as she remained at the Castelo she was duty bound to help Johnny, but if her job was finished he could not force her to stay. She would have to try and get everything completed in two days – three at the most. There lay the solution. And she must tell Carlos she would be returning to London very shortly.

Now that she had settled the problem in her mind, her spirits lifted and as she walked along the corridor her encounter with Johnny the night before seemed like a figment of her imagination. She was on the last stair when the library door opened and Carlos stepped out.

"Good morning. I thought I recognized your step."

"Did I disturb you?"

"Not at all." He came towards her. "If you're on your way to breakfast I'll join you."

They strolled out to the terrace and sat at the table in the corner.

"You're not usually up so early," he remarked as he helped himself to fruit. "Did a lovers' quarrel keep you awake?"

"Of course not!"

"Too much passion, then?" he suggested sarcastically.

"Not that either." Although she tried to keep her voice matter-of-fact, she felt warm colour seep into her face and applied herself to lavishly buttering a croissant.

"How long have you known Mr. Carlton?" he asked suddenly.

"I met him on the way out here. We – you know how it is with two English people in a foreign country. We were drawn together."

"Obviously. And do you think it's likely to last when you return home?"

"Who knows how long friendship lasts?" she said lightly.

In silence he picked up the newspapers by his plate and began to read. Looking at the heavy Portuguese lettering that headlined the front page brought home to Stephanie with unexpected force that the man sitting opposite her was a foreigner. How strange that she should be so drawn to him when they were so alien. Yet love knew no bounds. Love! How easily the word had sprung into her mind. She put down her half-eaten croissant and lowered her head. Sitting opposite Carlos, with his heavy eyebrows and aquiline nose, she admitted to herself that she loved him. Loved him without any logic, without any rhyme or reason. In a few days' time she would leave the Castelo far behind, but always she would have in her heart this strange, slightly sinister man whose only words to her were tinged with sarcasm, who had never kissed her or held her in his arms.

Putting down his paper, Carlos looked up. "What are you thinking about so seriously?"

"N-nothing," she stammered. "Just shoes and ships and sealing wax. That's from one of our English writers," she explained.

"Lewis Carroll," he replied. "It might surprise you to know I was educated in England. Eton, as a matter of fact."

Again she felt the colour flood into her face and wished she were not so vulnerable where he was concerned. "I'm sorry, I didn't know."

"There's no need to apologize. I've never known a girl change colour so many times." He leaned forward and rested his elbows on the table. "I would like to thank you, Stephanie. My mother told me this morning that you've been going to her room each evening and reading to her. It was very kind of you."

"Not at all: I enjoyed it. Your mother's charming."

"And her sons aren't?"

"I didn't say that. I think Miguel's extremely nice and – and so are you."

"For that little compliment I must return one." He pushed back his chair and Stephanie felt her pulse race as he came round the side of the table, but instead of stopping by her side he walked over to lean against the marble balustrade. Framed by the sunlight he looked unusually tall and dark, his white linen suit throwing into relief the wavy black hair and tanned skin.

"I've been thinking things over, Stephanie, and I've decided..." He paused, took a cigarette from his pocket and tapped it against his thumbnail. "I've decided to let you do the library. Miguel's right when he says it's shabby."

Wildly Stephanie sought for an excuse to refuse. If Carlos's capitulation had come a few days earlier how delighted she would have been at the prospect of staying longer at the Castelo. But the thought of being near him with Johnny's suspicions festering in her mind was something she could not endure.

"Why do you look like that?" Carlos asked. "Are you surprised that I should admit I was wrong?"

"A little," she admitted. "I was under the impression you never gave in once you'd made up your mind."

"Usually I don't," he answered candidly, "but with you a

lot of things are different. I want you to do the library for me, Stephanie, if only to keep you here a little longer."

She stood up so abruptly that her chair crashed to the floor and he came over and silently righted it.

"You're very nervous," he said quietly. "Are you afraid of me?"

"I don't know you well enough to be afraid of you." She looked at him and saw humour lurking in his eyes.

"Can I take that as an invitation to help you to get to know me better?"

Unused to subtle innuendoes, she was out of her depth. The young men with whom she spent her time in London had never treated her like this, at one moment aloof, the next disarmingly friendly. Because she was afraid, she kept her voice high so that it sounded cool and unemotional. "I'm sorry, Carlos, but I cannot stay in Portugal any longer. I've made all my arrangements to go home."

She knew by the expression on his face that he did not believe her.

"Then I'm afraid you'll have to cancel them," he said pleasantly. "You will stay here and complete your job, otherwise I will abandon the whole scheme."

"But you can't do that!"

"Oh yes, I can. And you know very well that I *will* if you don't obey me."

Anger sparked in her eyes and she tossed her head back sharply. "Your servant, sir!" she said and, turning her back, walked away.

She was crossing the drawing-room when Dinis came in. "Ah, *senhorita*, I was trying to find you. A letter has just arrived for you."

It was addressed in Felicity's handwriting and Stephanie opened it and glanced through the pages, giving an exclamation of surprise as she reached the end. Felicity was coming to Portugal with Robert!

I've got a fortnight's holiday owing to me, she had written, *and I don't fancy Bournemouth again. Robert's been working very hard since you went away and has decided he also needs a couple of weeks' break. So you can expect us both on the 14th. Our plane gets in at 2:30 p.m.*

The 14th! But that was today! Stephanie looked at the envelope again. No wonder it had been delayed in the post: Felicity had put the wrong town on it. She hurried to the telephone and dialled Johnny's number. Quickly she explained the position and her own difficulty.

"The letter's only just arrived and I haven't got a chance to find them any accommodation. I don't like bothering you, but if you could see whether they have any rooms available at your place . . ."

"Hang on a minute and I'll let you know."

Stephanie waited patiently and at last he came on the line again.

"You've no need to worry, old girl, it's all fixed up. Two rooms on the first floor have just fallen vacant and I've booked them for you."

"What an angel you are," she said gratefully and, replacing the receiver, turned round to find Carlos at her elbow. Nervously she crumpled the letter in her hand. "I was just talking to Johnny – Mr. Carlton."

"So I gathered." He looked at her from under lowered brows. "I'm sorry if I interrupted an intimate conversation."

Remembering her promise to Johnny and not wishing to dispel Carlos's belief that the young Englishman was in love with her, she checked the sarcastic reply that came to her lips.

"I've had a letter from my sister," she said coolly, "telling me she's coming here for a holiday and arriving today. The only trouble was that the letter was wrongly addressed and I didn't get it until just now. That's why I had to phone Johnny to see if he could fix accommodation at the inn where he's staying."

"I see. And was he able to arrange a room for her?"

"Two rooms," Stephanie corrected. "Robert's coming too."

He raised his eyebrows. "Who is Robert? Another of your lovers?"

"Certainly not," she said sharply. "He's my sister's boyfriend—" She stopped short, wondering what had made her tell the lie. But almost at once she realized that for Carlos to believe this would simplify matters all round. If he guessed that Robert was anxious to marry her, believing that Johnny was also in love with her, he would soon begin to put two and two together and wonder whether Johnny's love for her was a myth. Once this happened it would not take him long to arrive at the real reason for Johnny's breaking into the Castelo grounds.

"That's right," she added hurriedly. "They're engaged."

"So? I did not know you were having a wedding in your family soon. When is it to be – you will want to go home for it, no doubt."

"It isn't decided yet." Stephanie looked distractedly at her watch. Although there was plenty of time before the plane was due she was becoming nervous. It was imperative that she meet Felicity and Robert before they had a chance of coming to the Castelo to find her. If she didn't warn Robert of the situation he would certainly take her in his arms as soon as he saw her. And it would be just her luck that Carlos would be in the vicinity when he did so!

"If you'll excuse me," she said quickly, "I'd like to get through some work this morning so that I can go along to the airport after lunch."

"Naturally," Carlos said coldly. "You seem to think that you have to work fixed hours here. After lunch Manoel will take you to the airport in the car. You must invite your sister and her fiancé here for dinner during their stay."

"That's very kind of you."

"I don't intend to be kind," he said harshly. "But we Portuguese have a code of hospitality that we have to carry out whether we like it or not."

"And that," Stephanie thought as she looked at his retreating figure, "is that!"

Directly after lunch she set out for the long drive to Lisbon, arriving at the airport with fifteen minutes to spare. She lit a cigarette and glanced up into the deep azure sky, remembering her own arrival here a couple of weeks ago. How full of excitement she had been at the thought of what lay ahead of her. How she had woven romances around the Castelo and the Maroc family – and how differently everything had turned out. Romance, yes – but never had she imagined that to romance would be added intrigue, antagonism and the peculiar sense of secrecy that surrounded the family. Never had she imagined that she herself would get so involved in it all, that she would have to weave a web of pretence around herself that daily threatened to become more complex. She sighed and, looking up at the sky again, saw the glinting silver of the plane from London as it circled the airport preparatory to landing.

The leather seat hot against her legs, Felicity shifted and for the twentieth time craned out of the window. "We're actually here at last!" she exclaimed excitedly to the man beside her.

Robert leaned forward and looked out. "We'll be down in a minute – keep your seat belt fastened."

Felicity sighed happily. The journey with Robert had been blissful and the knowledge that they would be together for the next two weeks filled her with a happiness that she refused to analyse.

Robert looked at her, noticing the flush of excitement on her cheeks and the sparkle in her eyes. "It suits you to look excited, Felicity. Makes you quite pretty, in fact!"

The ungainly compliment jerked her back into reality, reminding her that it was her sister Robert loved. "Thanks," she said drily, "but you'd better keep your compliments for Stephanie. I don't happen to appreciate them."

Robert compressed his lips in annoyance. "What a prickly creature you are! *I* know you well enough not to mind your bad temper, but other men mightn't be so easy. If there's one thing they hate in a girl, it's sarcasm. If you don't learn to control your remarks now, one day you might find you've used them once too often on someone you're fond of!"

Felicity laughed. "But I'm not fond of anybody, nor likely to be."

"Don't talk like a child. You'll fall in love one day."

"No, I shan't," she answered. "Never!"

She spoke so emphatically that he was surprised, but made no reply, for the plane had already touched down and people were gathering their things and descending to the tarmac.

As Robert and Felicity walked out of the Customs shed, Stephanie ran towards them and threw her arms round her sister.

"Darling, how wonderful to see you. It's such a surprise – I only got your letter today."

"But I posted it last week!"

"I know – you put the wrong address on it, you idiot!"

They burst out laughing and hugged one another. "Never mind," Stephanie added. "You're here and I'm thrilled to bits."

"Hey!" said Robert plaintively. "Aren't you pleased to see me too?"

"Of course I am." Stephanie held out her hand, but he ignored it and pulled her into his arms.

"Robert, not here!" she protested. "Everyone can see. Besides, I want to talk to you first."

"And I want to kiss you first. It's a long time since I've seen you." He kissed her gently on the mouth and stepped back. "Now you can go ahead and talk – I don't mind."

Stephanie sighed and hoped that he wouldn't be too difficult when he heard what she had to say. "Let's go and have a coffee before we go along to the hotel. There's – there's something I want to tell you."

"You sound very mysterious!" Felicity remarked as she and Robert followed her to the airport bar.

"It's rather a long story," said Stephanie as she faced them across a small marble-topped table. "But I'd like to give you the outline now."

Briefly she told them how she had first met Johnny, of his interest in the Maroc Collection, the way she had caught him breaking into the Castelo grounds and the lie he had told to save himself.

"When he admitted he was a detective," she said, "I was completely bowled over. I had never imagined anything like that."

"But what was he looking for in the Castelo grounds?" Felicity asked.

"I don't know," Stephanie lied. "I suppose he was following some clue he'd got hold of, but he didn't tell me what it was. Anyway, I had to back him up when he pretended that he had come to meet me there, otherwise Carlos would have been furious."

"Carlos?" Robert raised his eyebrows.

Stephanie flushed. "It's easier than 'the Conde de Maroc.'"

Felicity laughed. "Shorter anyway! But I'm dying to know more about this mysterious detective and the stolen jewels he's looking for."

"I don't know any more than I've told you," Stephanie insisted. "All I know is that I've promised to help him by pretending he's my boy-friend. So I don't want you two to put your foot in it when you meet Carlos."

"It seems to me you're likely to land yourself in trouble," Robert put in. "I don't know that I care for this set-up at all."

"I don't care for it much myself," Stephanie agreed. "But I don't feel I can let Johnny down – after all, we're both English people in a foreign country."

"What's he like?" Felicity asked.

"You'll be meeting him soon. I've fixed up for you to stay at the same inn in Cintra. Oh, and there's just one other thing . . ." She swallowed, and avoiding Robert's eyes, looked at her sister. "I do hope you don't mind, darling, but I told the Conde that you and Robert were engaged."

Felicity caught her breath, but it was Robert who answered, his voice indignant. "What on earth did you want to do a thing like that for?"

"Because of Carlos. If he thought you had come to see *me*, he wouldn't believe that I was in love with Johnny. And then he'd wonder what Johnny was doing hanging about the Castelo grounds. It wouldn't take him long to put two and two together after that." Stephanie sighed and wished her sister and Robert had never decided to come to Portugal. "I'm sorry to implicate you two like this," she murmured. "But now you're here you've simply got to back me up."

"We've got no choice," Robert said grudgingly. "But I'm not pretending to like it."

Stephanie gave a sigh of relief and realizing it would be more diplomatic to say nothing further for the moment, stood up and led them outside to the car.

Felicity admired the sleek green Lagonda and the smart chauffeur holding the door open for them, and though Robert appeared to accept it as a matter of course, he too was secretly impressed. During the drive along the coast they chatted desultorily, and it was nearly five o'clock when they arrived at the inn, where Johnny was waiting for them.

After the introductions were made, Stephanie suggested that they go to their rooms and freshen up before coming down for a drink, and she followed Felicity upstairs to her bedroom, exclaiming in delight at the brightly painted walls, polished wooden floor and hooked rugs in vivid red and green.

"I've never been in a hotel room here before. Isn't it attractive?" She turned to her sister, stopping abruptly as she saw the expression on Felicity's face.

The girl was leaning against the bed, and catching her unawares, with her face in repose, Stephanie noticed how thin and pale she looked.

"Are you all right, darling?" she asked.

"Of course. Why?"

"You look so tired and you've got much thinner since I saw you last."

Felicity forced a smile. "I expect I'm just tired from the journey."

Stephanie hesitated. "I'm sorry about letting you in for this intrigue. Are you sure you don't mind pretending to be engaged to Robert while you're here?"

"It won't make much difference if I *do* mind," Felicity said. "If I'd had any idea of the real situation I would never have come."

"I didn't know myself till yesterday. If I could leave the Castelo, I would."

"*Would* you?" Felicity asked.

Stephanie shrugged. "Dad needs the money."

For a long moment the two sisters stared at one another, then Felicity turned away with a sigh and running her hands through her hair so that the front stood up in short tendrils, gazed out of the window.

Stephanie was consumed with sudden tenderness for her and tentatively put her hand on Felicity's arm. "I'm sorry, Lissa," she said. "I don't want this to spoil your holiday."

"That's O.K. Forget it."

"And you really won't mind pretending to be in love with Robert?"

Felicity turned away from the window. "I won't mind," she said slowly. "I won't mind at all."

After Stephanie had had a drink with Felicity and Robert, she left them to unpack their cases and returned to the Castelo.

"I've got a lot of work to get on with," she explained. "But I'll telephone and let you know which evening you can come up for dinner."

Driving away in the Lagonda she breathed a sigh of relief. She had not been looking forward to telling Robert and her sister the entanglements into which she had got herself, but it had gone off better than she had hoped. If only Johnny would find some clues that would take him to the other side of Europe, how happy she would be!

The car swung past the massive stone pillars and as it stopped outside the Castelo, she ran quickly up the steps to the house. Her head lowered, she did not see the man coming down until she bumped into him and he put out his hand to steady her.

"Hey!" he cried. "Where are you coming from in such a hurry?"

"I'm sorry! She looked up into Miguel's face. "Hello there. I thought you were still away."

"I got back an hour ago." He took her arm and walked with her into the drawing-room. "I'm flattered you should have noticed my absence! Especially as I've only been away three days."

"The Castelo is much quieter without you!"

He laughed. "I don't know whether to take that as a compliment or not. But you haven't answered my question. Where are you coming from in such a hurry?"

"Cintra. My sister and – and her fiancé have just arrived from England. They had a holiday due and decided to take it in Portugal – it's cheap here for English tourists, you know."

"A good thing too. It's time the South of France had some competition!" He let go her hands and reached into his pocket for a cigarette. "You're looking very pale, Stephanie, what's wrong with you?"

"I've been working too hard, I think." Abruptly she changed the subject. "Did you enjoy your trip?"

"I never like being away from home – and there's nothing enjoyable about inspecting a sardine factory!" He grinned. "But that's the price of owning one. The sardines earn us our bread and butter!"

"I don't believe that."

"Well, perhaps it's not strictly true." He looked down at her. "It's good to be here now that the Castelo is filled with beautiful women."

She smiled. "Only two!"

"That's enough for me. Carlos can occupy himself with Janique and I will concentrate on you."

Not feeling in the mood for any more flattery, she stepped past him, pausing as Janique came into the room.

"Miguel! So you're home again."

He walked over and raised her hand to his lips. "Just to see *you, amada*."

"I'm sure you said exactly the same thing to Stephanie!"

"Don't give away my secrets. I can see you know me too well." He put his arm across her shoulder. "Tell me, how much longer are you going to stay with us?"

"Does that mean you want me to go?"

"It's not up to *me*. If it were, you could stay here for ever."

Janique laughed, throwing back her head so that the white column of her throat swelled like the breast of a bird. "I'll stay here until I'm tired – and that might be tomorrow or a hundred tomorrows. It all depends on—" She paused, and Miguel raised an eyebrow.

"On what?"

"That's a secret."

A shadow darkened the doorway, breaking the sunbeams that danced their motifs on the carpet. "What's all this talk about secrets?" Carlos said. "Surely you two women aren't . . ." His voice trailed away as he saw Miguel. "So you're home again. I wondered when we were going to be honoured with the pleasure of your company."

"I had business to attend to, dear brother. You're not the only one who has to travel."

"I could end *my* travels if you would end *yours*."

Miguel smiled. "Think how dull that would be! I prefer it this way."

"No doubt you do, but you always have been foolhardy."

Miguel stubbed out his cigarette in an ash-tray. "You forget, Carlos, that our father was foolhardy, too, and I take after him."

"I don't think you're a bit like your father." Janique came into the conversation. "He was much more like Carlos than you."

"In looks maybe, but in temperament I'm sure Carlos will agree that he is not like my father at all."

Janique looked questioningly from one man to the other and Stephanie, sensing the tension, moved towards the door.

"Where are you going?" Carlos asked.

"I have work to get on with."

"Work!" Carlos burst out. "Do you ever think of anything else?" He looked as if he were about to say more, but seeing Janique's expression, contented himself with holding the door open for Stephanie. "I will talk to you later," he murmured.

"Is that an order?" she said softly.

"Carlos!" Janique interrupted them. "I want to talk to you."

Instantly he moved back from the door and Stephanie made her escape. She was half-way up the stairs when he called her name and she stopped, turning round hesitantly to see him framed in the doorway.

"I am going to show Janique the Collection later on. Would you like to see it as well?"

Although she would dearly have liked to say yes, some imp of perversity made her refuse, and as she shook her head, his expression hardened.

"You can't work all the time!"

"I know that. But I'm a little tired. I would prefer to rest."

"Then rest for half an hour now! I have some business to discuss with my brother until then. By the time we are ready to meet in the *salon* you will be feeling better."

Realizing it was impossible to refuse him again, she nodded her head and hurried upstairs. In the privacy of her room she relaxed, trying to puzzle out the reason for the brothers' mutual antagonism: that it existed was obvious, not only from what they said but in the way they looked at each other.

Last night, before she had known Felicity was arriving, she had decided that her only course was to return to England as soon as possible. Now Carlos himself had made that out of the question, for unless she stayed and completed the job he would cancel the whole commission.

Sighing, she stood up. Only when she left the Castelo would she find peace of mind. With all her heart she wished Johnny had never confided in her, for a confidence once given can never be forgotten, in the same way that suspicion once roused can never lie dormant.

Although she had told Carlos that she was going to rest, she found it impossible to do so, and with pad and ruler in hand, made her way to the library. It was not until her hand was on the door that she heard Carlos's voice raised in anger. Quickly she stepped back as she realized that the two brothers were quarrelling. How stupid of her! Carlos had said he was going to talk to Miguel and she might have known they would choose the library. Quickly she went upstairs again, but their voices still echoed through the hall and, without knowing why, she felt herself trembling as she ran into the *salon*.

The sight of Janique brought her to an abrupt halt, making her realize how untidy and unsophisticated she must look in her cotton dress, her face flushed from her precipitate flight up the stairs.

"Where's the fire?" Janique drawled. "Or have you had a quarrel with somebody?"

"I never quarrel," Stephanie said coldly.

"Of course. I'd forgotten that English people are always cool, calm and collected!"

Trying to ignore the undertone in Janique's remark, Stephanie sat down. Although wearing a plain tailored linen dress, the girl was the embodiment of sophistication, from the well-shod feet to the shining black hair twisted into a chignon on the nape of her graceful neck. It required little imagination to see her as the chatelaine of the Castelo and the mother of Carlos's children. The thought brought with it a moment of pain and Stephanie closed her eyes, opening them again as she recognized the heavy tread that mounted the stairs and entered the *salon*.

In silence Carlos took a key from his pocket, walked across the room and unlocked the large double doors at the far end. Flinging them open, he stepped inside and Stephanie followed, catching her breath at the magnificence of the long gallery. Although no more than twelve feet wide it stretched for some thirty feet: the numerous narrow windows curtained with dark gold velvet, the walls lined with embossed scarlet paper. Louis XV tables were ranged down either side and under the glass tops lay the fabulous pieces of the Maroc Collection.

Under Carlos's direction they walked to the bottom of the gallery and began to retrace their footsteps, pausing at each table to look at the various pieces. Stephanie had never imagined that such beauty existed, and she studied the intricate and delicate workmanship with awe. There was every jewel imaginable in the Collection, from jade to chalcedony, pearl to blue-white diamond. There were lockets and snuff-boxes designed by Fabergé, Renaissance style jewellery by Castellani and Fonteroy, as well as many examples of religious art worked in enamel, the brilliant reds and greens interspersed with hard blue and milk-white.

Watching Carlos as he bent to pick up a diadem or open a hand-beaten casket, she could see no emotion on his face, and wondered why the owner of this fantastic array of beauty should display such lack of pleasure in it. Could it be a guilty conscience? She pushed the thought aside and turned with a welcoming smile as Miguel came into the room.

"You don't know what a great honour this is," he remarked to Stephanie. "My brother rarely opens this room. Even for myself I have to beg the key." He sauntered over to a table and picked up a small enamelled umbrella handle of lapis lazuli embossed with gold. "I can just see some elegant countess in the Russian Court buying this to match her favourite walking suit." He minced along the narrow aisle, bowing first to the right and then to the left.

Stephanie could not help laughing at the impersonation of

a tightly corseted countess walking on the arm of a count and twisting an imaginary umbrella in her hand.

"Put it back, Miguel!" Carlos's voice rose across the laughter. "We've seen enough for today."

"Already? Have you shown Stephanie the emeralds?"

"No, I haven't."

"But my dear brother, why ever not! They are the same colour as her eyes. If you would like to wait a minute, Stephanie—"

"Miguel!" Carlos clamped his hand over his brother's face. The gesture was so rough that the younger man sprawled back against the table, his skin chalk white against Carlos's dark hand, still pressed over his mouth. For a long moment the two men looked at each other, then Carlos stepped back and Miguel took out a handkerchief from his breast pocket and slowly wiped his face.

"You should be more careful, brother. One day you'll be sorry for your impetuosity."

Tight-lipped with anger, Stephanie stepped forward. "I'd love to see the emeralds, Miguel," she said defiantly. But if she had expected him to show gratitude for her support, she was disappointed. As his colour returned, his nonchalance returned with it and he shrugged and smiled.

"Another time, my dear. There will be many more opportunities."

In the embarrassed silence Carlos turned on his heel and strode to the door. Without a word they all filed out and, uncomfortably aware of the tension, Stephanie hurried ahead.

"Do not disappear!" Carlos called. "Janique and I are going for a drive and I want you to come with us."

"I'd rather not, thank you." Again she saw the flame of anger in his eyes, but knew that because Janique and Miguel were with them, he would control himself. Taking advantage of their presence, she thanked Carlos for showing her the Collection and left.

Along the corridor she sped, intent only on reaching the

safety of her room and remaining there until Carlos and Janique left the Castelo. Up the short flight of steps she ran and along the narrow passage that led to her bedroom. Turning the corner, she ran full tilt into a pair of arms. With a cry she tried to draw back, but they closed like steel around her and, powerless to move, she looked up into Carlos's dark face.

"So!" he said softly. "At last I've managed to get you alone. I know that redheads are fiery-tempered, but I'd no idea you'd carry on the vendetta so long."

"I don't know what you're talking about."

"Don't know? How much longer are you going to make me suffer for what I said this morning?"

"I don't know what you mean."

"Of course you do," he said angrily. "Do you want me to grovel at your feet?" He stared at her and when she did not reply, he sighed. "I can see that you do. Very well then, I will grovel. It is not something that comes easily to me, you know."

"There's no need—" she began.

"But I want to apologize. I had no right to say what I did. But the knowledge that you wanted to leave the Castelo annoyed me so much that I spoke without weighing my words." He put his hands on her shoulders. They were heavy, their warmth penetrating the thin material of her dress. "You are free to go whenever you want to, Stephanie. I said what I did to you this morning because I didn't want you to leave – not from a desire to hurt you, as you seemed to think."

"I didn't know *what* to think," she admitted huskily. "This job means so much to my father . . ."

"I know it does," he replied. "And I'd never refute his bill – whether you went through with the job or not."

She did not reply and he tilted her chin, forcing her to look at him. "I can't make you out, Stephanie. At one moment your face is so candid – so open, and the next it is almost secretive, as if you are hiding something from me."

"I've nothing to hide."

"Not even your sudden friendship with Mr. Carlton?"

The moment he mentioned Johnny's name, Stephanie felt the colour leave her face and seeing it, Carlos dropped his hands from her shoulder. "What does he mean to you?" he asked harshly. "I *must* know what he means to you."

Desperately she longed to tell him the truth, but even as she wished it, she knew it was impossible to break her promise to Johnny. "He's a very good friend of mine."

"What exactly does that mean?"

She shrugged and before he could prevent her, pushed past him and ran along the corridor to her room. Closing the door, she leaned against it and stared in front of her. "Oh, Carlos," she murmured brokenly. "If only we had never met!"

CHAPTER SIX

STEPHANIE came down early for dinner that evening and entering the drawing-room, found the Condesa seated in the high-backed chair by the window. She was surprised at this for normally the old lady stayed in her room until the last moment, when either Miguel or Carlos escorted her downstairs.

"It was so hot," the Condesa explained as Stephanie came closer, "that I took a stroll in the garden. Come and sit next to me my child, and we can have a little chat."

Stephanie did as she was told and the Condesa picked up the piece of tapestry on which she was working. "What have you been doing with yourself today? If I'm not mistaken I believe I saw you go out in the car this afternoon?"

"My sister and her fiancé arrived from England; I went to the airport to meet them."

"That must have been exciting for you. I hope you have asked them here for dinner tonight."

Stephanie was taken by surprise and sensing it, the old lady smiled.

"But naturally you will want to have your sister and her fiancé here to visit you. I should imagine that is one of the reasons they have come to Portugal. They probably wanted to see how you are getting on amongst us barbaric foreigners."

Stephanie grinned. "I wouldn't dare to agree with you over that! But my being here certainly gave them the incentive to come."

"Then you must ring them up at once and invite them for dinner."

Stephanie hesitated. "Tonight?"

"Of course."

"But what will Carlos—"

"*I* am issuing the invitation," the Condesa said decisively. "Now run along and telephone them. Dinner won't be served for another hour and I'm sure they can be here well within that time."

Realizing the futility of arguing with the autocratic old woman, Stephanie went into the hall and in a few moments was speaking to her sister.

"But it's such short notice," Felicity complained. "And I'm not even half ready."

"It won't take long to change," Stephanie placated, "and a taxi can bring you up here within twenty minutes. You'd better come, Felicity, the Portuguese code of etiquette is pretty strict and I don't want to offend the old girl."

"Very well. I must admit I'd like to see the Castelo and its owner. I'll go and tell Robert."

By the time Stephanie returned to the drawing-room both the brothers were already there and Carlos came forward with a drink.

"My mother has just told me we are having guests for dinner tonight."

Stephanie took the glass from him. "I hope you don't mind."

"On the contrary. I am looking forward to meeting them."

"So am I," Miguel drawled. "If your sister is anything like you she must be a beauty."

Carlos turned away with compressed lips and to cover her embarrassment Stephanie said quickly, "I do hope they won't be late. I don't want to keep you waiting."

"We're used to being kept waiting," Miguel interrupted again. "I've never known a more unpunctual woman than Janique."

"Who's taking my name in vain?"

They turned to see Janique in the doorway. In a black dress that fitted her figure like a sheath, she looked as

103

glamorous as any film star and equally aware of it. "I always set out with the intention of being punctual," she explained, "but every time I do, something goes wrong." She came forward and, kissing the Condesa on the cheek, took a chair beside her. "I didn't realize it was so late though. I hope I haven't kept you waiting longer than usual?"

"Tonight is one occasion when it doesn't matter," Carlos said. "We're expecting some more guests to arrive."

"Oh really? Who?"

"Miss North's sister and her fiancé."

"Indeed." Janique turned to Stephanie. "Is your sister anything like you?"

"I don't think so. She isn't quite as tall as I am and has brown hair and blue eyes."

"Brown hair and blue eyes," Janique repeated. "That sounds as if we will have two English beauties in the Castelo this evening."

The tone in which she spoke ensured that the remark could not be construed as a compliment and Stephanie was trying to think of a suitable retort when the door opened and her sister and Robert came in.

Felicity was wearing a cream dress Stephanie had not seen before; she had left her glasses off and, with her face flushed from hurrying and the excitement of seeing the Castelo, was looking unusually pretty. Robert too seemed more handsome than Stephanie had remembered and she hurried forward to greet them, stopping short as a third figure followed the other two into the room. Johnny Carlton! Stephanie flushed with anger at his audacity and her fingers itched to slap the grin off his innocent-looking face.

Not daring to look at Carlos, she murmured introductions, but in spite of herself her eyes sought his face. He was glaring at her in such anger that she hastily turned away and lifted her glass to her lips. Unfortunately it was empty and Carlos seized the opportunity to come over to her with the decanter.

"I wasn't aware Mr. Carlton was included in the invitation this evening." His tone was quiet.

"I'd no idea he was going to come," she said nervously. "I didn't ask him."

"You don't expect me to believe that!"

"But it's true!"

"Don't lie!" he said harshly. "Even Mr. Carlton wouldn't have the impudence to come to dinner uninvited."

Furiously she looked him in the face. "I'm not used to being called a liar, Conde. If you'd like me to—"

The rest of her words were drowned as the dinner gong reverberated through the hall, and immediately Carlos stepped back and proffered his arm to his mother.

Slowly they filed across the hall to the dining-room and on the threshold Stephanie glanced at her sister, amused at the awe on Felicity's face as she looked at the long polished table with its heavy silver and glassware sparkling in the light of tall red candles. The air was scented with bowls of deep crimson roses which marked their places and as the women took their seats, servant girls came forward and presented each one with a corsage of gardenias.

To begin with, conversation at the table was constrained, but as the white wine was replaced by red, the tempo changed. Miguel was at his most high-spirited and Janique, always at her best with an audience, responded to his banter. Robert engaged in a spirited conversation with Felicity, occasionally making a deferential remark to the Condesa, while Stephanie, still annoyed with Carlos, defiantly set herself out to be particularly attentive to Johnny, who needed no further encouragement to respond to her. Only Carlos sat silent, a dark look on his face as he answered all questions monosyllabically and played with the stem of his wineglass.

The meal was a long one and by the time it was over and they had finished their coffee, it was nearly midnight. Felicity followed her sister's glance to the ormolu clock that stood on the mantelshelf and interpreting the movement correctly, touched Robert's arm.

But Robert was talking to the Condesa, who was telling him about the places of interest to tourists in Portugal.

"I will be very pleased to lend you my car and chauffeur any time you wish," she said graciously.

"That's most kind of you," Robert said. "I may take you up on the offer. I've heard Estoril is your most popular seaside resort."

"And the smartest too," the Condesa said. "It's only an hour's journey away."

Robert straightened in his chair and looked at Stephanie. "What do you say to going along there tonight? We could all pile into your car, couldn't we, Johnny? It's been such a wonderful evening it seems a pity to break it up now."

"I couldn't agree more," Johnny replied, glancing at Stephanie for approval.

Although Stephanie's main desire was to go to sleep, she was so relieved at the thought of getting Johnny away from the Castelo that she would have agreed to anything, and she hurried upstairs to fetch her coat. When she came down again they were gathered in the hall and to her dismay Carlos and Janique were with them.

Seeing her expression, he smiled mockingly. "I hope you don't mind if Janique and I join your party?"

"Of course not."

"I know we should have waited for an invitation," he went on smoothly. "But I wasn't sure we'd get one!"

"You are very welcome to come," she said stiffly, and marched out the door to Johnny's car.

The Mercédès, with Robert and Felicity in the back, swept ahead of them, and alone with Johnny for the first time that evening, Stephanie turned on him furiously.

Before she could speak he held up his hand. "I know what you're going to say, but I can't have a row with you while I'm driving. Must concentrate on the road, you know."

"I'm afraid you'll have to concentrate on me as well! Of all the rotten things you've done, coming along here tonight was the worst."

"I didn't like doing it," he conceded. "I know it put you in an awkward position."

"Awkward!" Her voice rose. "That's the biggest understatement of the year. Carlos and the Condesa thought I invited you without asking them. It made me look an ill-mannered boor."

"Well, you've got my permission to tell them I gate-crashed."

"I did, don't worry! But Carlos wouldn't believe me."

"I'm sorry," he said again. "But you know how important it is to me. When Felicity and Robert said they were coming to dinner I simply couldn't miss the opportunity."

"It doesn't seem to have done you much good."

"Yes, it has. It's got me on familiar terms with the Marocs – and, who knows, next time I might get a *bona fide* invitation!"

"Don't you believe it! Carlos is furious with you as well as with me. And I don't blame him."

"Well, it's done now and it's no good beefing at me all the evening. You're supposed to be my girl-friend, remember? If you don't give a better imitation of love's young dream, his high and mightiness will think we're pulling a fast one on him about that too."

"Oh, Johnny, you're impossible!" In spite of her anger, Stephanie could not help an unwilling smile at his impudence. "I suppose I'll have to forgive you, but don't ever do anything like it again."

"I promise." He took his hand from the wheel and pressed it over hers. "You're a nice girl, Stephanie. One day I hope to be able to elaborate on that." He peered through the window. "What are we supposed to do once we get to Estoril?"

"Knowing Carlos, I'd say he's probably got something in mind."

She was proved right, for when they arrived at the seaside town, the Mercédès turned left at the Palace Hotel and drove up the hill to the Casino, a large white building set amidst trees. Carlos was evidently well known, for the commissionaire bowed him in without asking to see his card and they followed him across the marble-floored hall to the gaming rooms.

It was crowded and hot, and people jostled each other to get to the tables. There were far more men than women, and a sprinkling of the inevitable *demimondaine*, all of them wearing numerous gold bracelets and gold rings, as if this were a sign of their profession.

Stephanie's eyes smarted in the smoky atmosphere and she rubbed them surreptitiously with her hand. Almost as if it were a signal, Carlos suggested they adjourn to the ballroom where he had booked a table, and even though Janique protested that she was winning and wanted to go on playing, he obdurately refused to remain in the gaming *salon* any longer.

"Stay and play by all means," he said suavely. "In fact, I'm sure Mr. Carlton will be delighted to remain here and look after you."

"I'd be honoured," Johnny replied promptly, and winked at Stephanie as she walked past him.

The ballroom was equally crowded, but the windows overlooking the terrace were wide open and a waiter led them to a large table in the corner.

Stephanie sat down and watched the couples on the vast polished floor beneath the magnificent chandeliers.

"Will you dance with me, Stephanie?"

She looked up to see Carlos's dark face close to hers and without a word rose and followed him on to the floor. For an instant nervousness made her stumble, but as he placed his hand on her waist, she gave herself up to the joy of being in his arms. Their steps matched perfectly and she sighed and thought how blissful this moment might have been if only things had been different between them.

Hearing the sigh, Carlos pressed her closer, but did not speak. Their bodies moved in perfect rhythm and Stephanie closed her eyes and rested her forehead against his cheek. She heard him murmur something and felt the rhythm of his step change, but it was not until a breath of cool air on her cheek made her open her eyes that she found he had guided her out on to the balcony.

He turned and faced her, leaning his back against the balustrade. The moonlight glimmered on her red hair, lighting the ends so that they formed a nimbus round her head. Her skin shone pale and the soft material of her dress clung to the delicate curves of her body.

"You're so beautiful," he whispered, but although his voice was husky with passion his lips were set in a tight, hard line. "You've no right to be so lovely and yet—"

"And yet what?" she demanded.

Without answering he reached out and pulled her roughly into his arms. Ignoring her struggles, he bent his head until his mouth touched hers. She tried to pull away, but he would not let her go, forcing her lips open with his seeming to draw the very strength from her body. His arms closed more tightly round her and he kissed her eyes and her hair, murmuring softly in Portuguese.

"Carlos, no!" she panted. "Leave me alone."

But still he took no notice and she went limp in his hold. Instantly he eased his grip, but as he did so, she pushed away from him and stepped back, smoothing her hair with trembling fingers, pulling at the bodice of her dress where it had torn in her struggles to be free.

"You – you had no right to do that," she whispered. "No right to insult me."

"I'm sorry." His voice was so low that she could barely hear it. "But if ever a woman asked for it, you did."

"I don't know what you mean."

"Don't play the innocent with me! All the evening you've tried to make me jealous by flirting with your Mr. Carlton."

"I've no desire whatsoever to make you jealous," she lied. "There's no point in pretending that I'm not friendly with Johnny. You know the way we feel about each other and—"

"I know the way Mr. Carlton feels about *you*. But I'm not

sure how you feel about *him* – particularly after the way in which you kissed me."

Afraid that if she answered she might give herself away, she turned on her heel and went back into the ballroom, threading her way through the tables to the cloakroom. It was only as she put her bag down on the marble ledge and looked at herself in the mirror that she saw Janique combing her hair at the far end of the room. Their eyes met in the glass and the French girl turned round.

"You're looking somewhat the worse for wear," she remarked. "What have you been up to?"

Stephanie shrugged and Janique's voice grew sharper. "I asked you a question, Miss North."

"And I chose not to answer it."

Janique's eyes narrowed until they were mere slits in her face. "So the English crudeness is coming to the surface at last. I wondered how long it would be before you showed yourself in your true colours."

Stephanie clenched her hands, but refused to lose her temper. "You are not my keeper," she said gently, "and I don't have to tell you what I do. If you don't mind, I'd like you to leave me alone."

"It's not for *me* to leave *you* alone," Janique said through clenched teeth. "It's for you to leave Carlos alone! Don't think I'm not aware of what you're up to. I know the game you're playing at, and the sooner you leave the Castelo and go back to your own country the better it will be for you. I'm an easy-going person, Miss North, but there's one thing I won't tolerate – and that's other people putting their hands on my property."

For the second time that evening Stephanie was too angry to speak and afraid that if she lost her temper she might do something she would regret, she swung round and ran from the room. Outside the ballroom she paused to regain control of herself and as she went back inside, saw with relief that Johnny was alone at the table. Felicity and Robert were dancing and there was no sign of Carlos.

She sat down in her chair and reached for a cigarette. "I don't want to spoil your evening, Johnny, but I've had enough of it here. Could you take me home?"

Instantly he got to his feet. "Sure. What about the others?"

"They can go back in Carlos's car."

At that moment Robert and Felicity returned to the table and Stephanie told her sister that she was returning to the Castelo. "I want to get up early and hurry on with some work," she said. "Then I'll feel more free to spend a few hours with you during the day."

"We might as well come back with you too." Robert said.

Stephanie shook her head. "You came with Carlos, so you'd better return with him."

Robert looked as if he wanted to disagree, then seeing the entreaty on her face, shrugged. "Very well, old girl. But you know what I'd rather do, don't you?"

She squeezed his hand and then preceded Johnny out of the casino to the car.

As soon as Stephanie left the ballroom Felicity sensed a change in Robert, and when they started to dance again she had the feeling that he was giving her his full attention for the first time that evening.

"Do you know you're a very good dancer?" he remarked as they danced together. "I'd have thought you'd be too inhibited to do this sort of thing."

"I could have said the same about you."

"Really?" He was surprised. "But I'm a very good dancer. Didn't Stephanie tell you?"

"I never discuss you with Stephanie."

He grinned. "You needn't rub it in."

"Rub what in?" Felicity looked up.

"The fact that you couldn't care less about me."

She didn't reply and he pulled her a little closer.

"At least you're learning," he murmured into her ear. "The old Felicity would have made some sharp come-back, but the new one knows when to maintain a discreet silence!"

It was nearly three o'clock before the Mercédès slid to a stop outside the inn and, thanking Carlos for their lovely evening, Felicity and Robert walked into the lobby.

"I feel as if I've been here for days," she yawned, "and yet it isn't even twenty-four hours yet."

"I feel the same," he agreed. "I suggest we call it a night."

Together they walked upstairs and saying good night in the corridor, went to their respective rooms.

It did not take Felicity long to undress and, slipping on a dressing-gown, she made her way sleepily to the bathroom. Returning to her room, she switched on the light and as she did a large bat which had flown through the window and settled on the lampshade flapped blindly towards her. Terrified, she gave a piercing shriek and almost before it died away the door was flung open and Robert rushed in.

"What on earth's the matter, Felicity?"

Speechlessly she waved her hand towards the bat and he burst out laughing. Then, seeing she was really afraid, he set to work to chase it out the window, closing it firmly behind him when he had succeeded. "There you are. It can't get in again."

She did not answer and, coming close, he saw she was still shaking. "I tell you, it's all right. You needn't be afraid any more."

"I know I'm a fool," she whispered, "but I can't bear them."

"Poor little thing." Putting his arm round her, he stroked her hair and murmured comforting words as if she were a child.

Weak with relief, Felicity leaned against him and, as he felt her slim body and smelled the fragrance of her hair, it was suddenly no longer a little girl he was holding in his arms, but a woman – a young, desirable woman. Without thinking his arms tightened round her and, raising her face, he kissed her warmly on the mouth.

Felicity's eyes closed and her lips were pliant under his, but as memory returned, and afraid that her momentary response had given away her feelings for him, she drew back and smacked him sharply across the face.

White with anger, Robert glared down at her, then putting out his hands, pulled her roughly back into his arms. This time his kiss was long and passionate and Felicity had no opportunity to draw away. Again and again he pressed his mouth on hers until at last, exhausted, he let her go.

"My God," he gasped. "I – I don't know what got into me. I'm sorry, Felicity, I – I'll never do it again."

Turning her back on him she pressed a hand to her mouth. "You'd better go," she said huskily. "And for God's sake don't mention it in the morning again."

Robert stared at the slim shoulders turned away from him and then slowly walked to the door.

In his own room he sank down on the bed and stared in front of him. "I must have been crazy," he said aloud. "Why on earth did I have to go and kiss her?" And for the first time he asked a question to which he did not know the answer.

CHAPTER SEVEN

STEPHANIE slept most of the way during her drive back to the Castelo in Johnny's car and only opened her eyes as they screeched to a stop in the curving driveway.

"I'm not going to ask you to invite me in for a drink," he said humorously as he escorted her to the front door. "I think I've tried my luck far enough for one night."

"You can say that again!" she agreed, and pressed the bell.

"How come you don't have a key?" Johnny asked.

"No one has keys to the Castelo. There are night watchmen in the grounds as well as the guard dogs and one of the servants is always on duty in the hall."

"That must make it rather like a prison," he remarked. "Doesn't it get you down?"

"It would if I thought about it," she admitted, "but it's amazing how quickly one gets used to having people around all the time."

"It makes my job even more difficult, of course," he said slowly. "The Collection must be very well guarded. Even when it was on show in Paris, Carlos brought his own private detectives along as a safeguard."

"I'm not surprised. It's the most magnificent thing I've ever seen."

"Do you mean you've seen it?" Johnny seized her arm. "You never told me! What was it like?"

"I could never describe it all to you, but I did look out to see if there was anything unusual."

"I take it there wasn't?"

She nodded. "Even if there were, I don't think I could have remembered."

"Yes, you would," he said gravely. "If they'd got hold of the sort of things I'm looking for, you'd never forget them once you saw them."

His words tinged her with fear and she said quickly, "I told you I'd never play detective for you. I'm not cut out to be a spy, Johnny."

He opened his mouth to say something, but the massive door behind them creaked open and thankfully Stephanie slipped into the house.

Up in her room she gazed through the window at the moonlit garden and watched the tail-light of Johnny's car disappear before turning towards the bed. But she was too restless to sleep and decided to go downstairs again and get some magazines she had seen in the drawing-room.

The room was in darkness when she entered it and without bothering to switch on the light, she went over to the side table where the books lay. She was about to pick one up when a sound at the French windows made her swing round and she saw Carlos stepping in from the terrace.

"Who's there?" he said loudly.

"M-me – Stephanie," she stammered. "I was looking for something to read. I don't feel like sleeping."

"I hope I'm not the cause of your insomnia?" He came towards her and she noticed how pale he was. "I owe you an apology, Stephanie. I had no right to behave the way I did to you tonight. I'm afraid my . . ." he hesitated and when he continued his voice was even and expressionless, "I'm afraid my Latin temperament got the better of me."

"Please don't talk about it any more."

"But I must. I've put you in an awkward position. I'm your employer, but I would like you to know that no matter what happened between us, I won't let it affect your job here."

"I'm glad of that," she said and, turning away, picked up the magazine.

He stepped close to her and she could feel his breath warm on the nape of her neck. "There's one more thing," he said quietly. "I would like you to know that I will no longer bother you with unwanted attentions. I made a mistake in thinking there was an affinity between us. It's obvious to me that Mr. Carlton is more suited to you than I am."

With all her heart Stephanie wished she were free to tell him how wrong he was. But to say this would mean explaining far more than she was at liberty to do. How could she tell him that Johnny suspected him of being a thief? She clenched her hands so tightly against the magazine that the edge of the paper cut into her skin. Carlos was not guilty! Every moment she spent with him convinced her of that. If only there was something she could say that would give him comfort.

"Don't look so worried," he murmured. "There's no need for you to find a sop for my vanity. I realize it is impossible for a man and woman of a different race to come together."

With difficulty she made herself answer. "You always knew that. I remember you saying so to Miguel."

"I say many things to Miguel," he replied harshly, "but I do not necessarily believe them. Until tonight I thought that if a love was sufficiently strong it could overcome everything, even the barriers of race and language."

"And what – what made you change your mind?"

"Seeing your sister and her fiancé together," he said wearily. "They seem to have so much in common – they laugh at the same jokes and innuendoes." He took a cigarette from his case, lit it and snapped the match between his fingers. "I can see that my mother is right after all. When I choose a wife she will have to be of my own country – or at least of the Latin race."

Suddenly Stephanie could no longer bear the conversation and murmuring an incoherent good night, slipped past him.

In her room again she flung herself on the bed and buried her head in her arms. Carlos had told her as plainly as possible that Janique would be a more suitable wife for him than she herself. Yet what right did she have to assume that even if he did not marry Janique, he would want her instead? A few compliments and a few kisses should not be regarded as a declaration of love. Passion maybe, but certainly nothing more.

In the morning Stephanie went round all the upstairs rooms, checking her work and making sure she had not missed out anything. The only room left untouched was the library, but she was reluctant to start work on it, for when she did so she would be unable to avoid meeting the family, and at the moment she did not feel capable of making conversation with anyone – particularly Carlos.

Even when lunchtime came she pleaded a headache and asked for her meal to be brought to her room. When it arrived she pushed it listlessly about on her plate and wished that her work were completed and she was able to leave the Castelo.

"I'm darned if I'll start on the library today," she said aloud. "If I give myself a few hours off I'm sure to feel better."

Without giving herself a chance to change her mind she went downstairs to telephone her sister and arranged to go down to the inn for tea. Flinging a jacket over her shoulders, she set off for the long walk and was half-way down to the village when she sighted Robert walking towards her.

"Quite a steep climb," he murmured, mopping his brow. "I can see now why they have such good brakes on their cars!"

Slowly she strolled along the lane and, walking by his side, Stephanie felt as if she were home again. It gave her a feeling of contentment she had not experienced since her arrival in Portugal and she wondered whether, when she were back in England amongst the friends and atmosphere she knew, her love for Carlos would disappear. Trying to convince herself that it would, she became more light-hearted and Robert responded to her mood, teasing her gently, making her laugh with unexpected jokes so that the rest of their walk was completed far more quickly than she had realized.

Felicity and Johnny were seated at a table on the terrace overlooking the square. They seemed to be enjoying a private joke together and Stephanie watched in surprise as her sister put her hand on Johnny's arm to emphasize a remark she had made. Such a gesture of familiarity with a man she had known a short time was strange in so reserved a girl, and Stephanie wondered if her sister had fallen in love with the young detective. But it was unlike Felicity to give her heart as quickly as all that and Stephanie watched them, puzzled. She glanced at Robert and noticed that he too was watching Felicity with an irritated, half-anxious expression.

Tea over, the four of them moved farther back on the terrace to sit in the shade of the wall. Robert busied himself with deck-chairs and Johnny, murmuring that he was out of cigarettes, went off to get some.

As soon as he was out of sight, Robert turned to Felicity. "Don't you think you're making a bit too much of a play for that chap?"

Felicity flushed. "I don't know what you're talking about."

"That surprises me." Disregarding the ominous glint in her eyes, Robert blundered on. "If I didn't know you so well I'd have said you were throwing yourself at him."

"Whose business is it if I am? I think I told you once before that whatever I do is no concern of yours. In other words, Robert, mind your own business!"

Pushing back her chair, Felicity stalked into the hotel and Stephanie was unable to suppress a smile at the look of amazement on Robert's face.

"You asked for that," she said gently. "Felicity's free to do as she likes."

"But you saw yourself the way she was behaving."

"So what? There's no harm in a mild flirtation. Anyway, Johnny's a nice person. If he and Felicity *did* fall in love—" She broke off as Johnny sauntered towards them, cigarettes in hand.

"How about a bit of sightseeing? We've been in Cintra all this time yet we haven't seen the Palace."

"Good idea," Robert said over-hurriedly, and turned to Stephanie. "You'd better go and tell Felicity."

"I've already told her," Johnny replied, "and she's gone to get her glasses."

Robert stood up and held out his hand to Stephanie. "In that case we might as well walk ahead."

For the next hour they wandered through the Palace, studying the beautiful pictures that lined the walls and the lovely antiques that furnished the main rooms. Wandering along together, Robert and Stephanie found themselves alone in a small ante-room, and she touched her fingers admiringly down one of the brocade curtains.

"How beautiful this must have been years ago," she murmured. "I wish I could have seen it in all its glory."

Robert nodded, but his eyes were on her face. "You're the only glory that I want to see. Oh, Stephanie . . ." He caught her hand. "Stephanie, when are you going to marry me?"

"Robert, don't." She tried to pull away from him. "Please don't ask me again. I told you in England that I didn't love you—"

"I know, but I keep hoping you'll change your mind. I warned you that I'd go on proposing until you did."

"I wish you wouldn't. I don't love you and I never will."

"You seem pretty sure."

"I am." She hesitated. "If I were going to fall in love with you, I've had plenty of opportunity. Maybe I know you too well. Maybe it's just fate that—"

"Your fate is what you make it, Stephanie."

"Then maybe I don't want to make my fate with yours."

The words came out more harshly than she had intended and seeing him change colour, she was instantly sorry for what she had said. But it was better to be truthful even if it hurt him, for there would only be more hurt for him if he persisted in his belief that they would eventually marry.

"I'm sorry, Robert," she said gently. "But you do see what I mean, don't you?"

"I'd be blind if I didn't." He let her hand go. "I seem to make a mess of everything I do. You and Felicity—"

"Don't take any notice of Felicity. She'll soon forget what you said today."

"It's not only today." He put his hands in his pockets and looked at the ground. "I'm afraid I had a bit of a row with her last night too."

"I can't see you pretending to be an engaged couple for long," she said drily.

"Neither can I. But I'll certainly do my best to oblige you."

Relieved that the conversation was no longer personal, Stephanie glanced at her watch. "I think I'd better be getting back to the Castelo. I won't wait for the others to come along. I'll see if I can pick up a taxi in the village."

Together they left the Palace and descended the steep stone steps to the square. A line of ancient taxi-cabs was parked by the fountain and Robert put Stephanie into one, making her promise that she would telephone him the following day. He watched until the cab swung round the square and then disappeared up the steep road that led to the hill before he strolled back to the inn.

He glanced at the terrace and into the lounge, but there was no sign of Felicity and illogically annoyed, he decided to go to his room and read until dinner. Turning a bend in the corridor, he saw Felicity and Johnny standing outside her room. She was laughing and as though to stop her, Johnny bent his head and planted a kiss on her mouth. She gave a little push in protest, but by the way she continued to smile, it was obvious she was not in the least bit disturbed by the kiss. Furiously angry, Robert pushed past them and slammed the door of his room.

"What on earth's got into him?" Johnny exclaimed. "Fancy pushing past us like that."

"Don't mind Robert," Felicity said carelessly. "He always was moody."

"Maybe he's jealous of you."

"Jealous of me!" She tossed her head. "Fat chance I've got of that."

But later, as she lay on the bed smoking a cigarette, she wondered whether Johnny could be right. Why should Robert mind if he saw her kissing another man? In London he had continually teased her because she had no boy-friends and even on their journey out here he had jokingly remarked that he hoped she would meet a tall, dark handsome foreigner. But she had met a charming Englishman instead and it had obviously annoyed him.

With a sudden lightening of spirits she decided that a good dose of jealousy might not be a bad thing for him after all.

She was still pondering on this when a maid entered and told her she was wanted on the telephone. Knowing it could only be Stephanie, she ran quickly downstairs.

"I'm sorry I couldn't wait to say good-bye to you this afternoon," her sister said, "but I had to get back to the Castelo."

"That's O.K. Johnny's a wonderful guide and we did the Palace from end to end!"

"Well, I hope you're not too tired to come and have dinner with me tonight. I want to talk to you and I've arranged for us to dine alone. Unless of course you don't want to leave Robert."

"It'll do him good to be by himself," Felicity remarked cheerfully, and rang off.

Stephanie put the receiver down at her end, a surprised look on her face. There was no doubt that Felicity was coming out of her shell!

The two girls ate their evening meal in the little breakfast-room overlooking a walled *patio* at the side of the Castelo. It was the first time they had been on their own since Felicity's arrival in Portugal and Stephanie found it a relief to be completely natural.

"There's so much protocol here," she explained, "that I feel as if I'm walking on eggs all the time, as if something's going to explode."

"Maybe it's because you know Johnny's a detective."

"Possibly. It's put me in an awfully difficult position."

"I don't see why. If Johnny's right then I hope he catches the crooks, and if he's wrong . . ."

"I'm not worrying about what will happen if he's wrong," Stephanie retorted. "But if the Marocs *are* guilty—" She pushed back her chair and walked over to the window, staring out at the flowering tubs that half covered the mosaic-tiled floor. "I'm so miserable, Lissa," she burst out. "I've simply got to tell someone the way I feel. I – I'm in love with Carlos!"

"What!" Felicity pushed back her own chair and hurried over to her sister's side. "Stephanie, you're not, you can't be!"

"Well, I am. And it's no good you trying to talk me out of it, because I've tried to talk myself out of it and it doesn't help."

"It's just infatuation," Felicity said. "He's handsome and very wealthy and so different from all the other men we know that I could almost fall in love with him myself."

"It's not infatuation." Stephanie blinked her eyes to hold back the tears. "I know he's good-looking and I know he's rich, but it goes deeper than that. When he comes into a room I feel as if I'm alive and when he walks out I might just as well stop breathing. There's so much about him that I love – the way he talks, the way his mind works, his outlook on everything."

"But he's so different from us! You'd be crazy to marry him without giving yourself a chance to find out a bit more about him. Saying Johnny's right—"

"I'm sure he's not. And anyway, you needn't look so worried. I don't stand a chance with Carlos. He's as good as told me he's going to marry Janique."

"Then you've got to get away. I'm not going to let you stay here and pine for a man who's stupid enough to prefer that conceited snob to you. For goodness' sake get shot of the job and leave. Once you're away from the Castelo, Johnny can stew in his own juice. He had no right to drag you into his affairs. I don't care if he's the head of the C.I.D. himself!"

"I've got to do the library before I go. If I left the job uncompleted I'd be letting Dad down."

"He wouldn't mind if I explained—"

"You're not to! I don't want anyone to know the way I feel. Felicity, promise me."

Felicity sighed. "Very well. But I don't like the idea of leaving you alone here." She moved back to the table and sat down again. "I can't say I'll be sorry to get back home either."

"But I thought you were enjoying yourself."

Felicity was silent for a moment, then gave a forced laugh. "Since we seem to be letting our hair down I might as well do the job properly and tell you *my* secret." She looked down at her plate. "I'm in love with Robert. I've been in love with him for years."

Stephanie stared at her sister in amazement. "What a fool I've been not to have realized it before! Oh, darling, it must have been awful for you. When I think of the times I spoke about him, the details I went into. I'd had no idea—"

"Don't worry about it. You'd be surprised how tough I got about the whole thing. I wouldn't have told you even now if I thought there was a chance of your marrying him, but I realize you never will."

"I hope to heaven *he* does! I tried to make it clear again this afternoon." Stephanie poured the coffee the maid had left in a small percolator. "How would it be if I dropped a hint to Robert about the way you feel?"

"I'd never forgive you if you did – never!"

"I was only trying to help."

Felicity put down her cup abruptly. "I know you were, but I couldn't bear it."

"All right. I won't say a word."

As if by common consent the subject was changed and they chatted desultorily until Felicity decided it was time to leave. The Condesa had left instructions for Manoel to run her back in the car and not wishing to keep him up late, they said goodnight soon after they finished their dinner.

It was still too early to go to bed and Stephanie sat by her bedroom window and looked out into the garden. She was in time to see Carlos and Janique drive away in the Mercédès and she wondered if they were going to Estoril again. She visualized the French girl sitting close to him in the car, her hand resting on his knee as he drove. The thought was anguish and she closed her eyes, feeling the salt of tears on her lips.

Footsteps echoed below her and, lifting her head, she looked through the window again. Miguel was strolling along the terrace and as she watched, he vaulted the balustrade and running lightly over the grass, opened the door to a small sports car parked by a clump of trees. A moment later he too disappeared down the drive.

Chin on hands, she remained staring out of the window at the garden shimmering silver in the moonlight. Sleep seemed farther away than it had ever been and sighing, she moved away and closed the casement. Felicity was right: only when the Castelo was far behind her would she find peace of mind, and the sooner the job was completed the better.

She began to undress but suddenly stopped, struck by a sudden thought; surely, rather than lying sleepless in bed, it would be better to start work on the library? Quickly she put on a pair of house-shoes, picked up her pad and ruler and went downstairs. The house was hushed and most of the lights had been turned out, leaving only a few lamps placed at strategic intervals along the corridor and stair well.

She pushed open the library door and went in. Again she was struck by the beauty of the octagonal-shaped room and the large alcove with its alabaster figures. There was very little that she could do here beyond suggesting a slightly deeper colour scheme and perhaps the removal of two bookcases on either side of the alcove. They were too heavy, she thought, and wondered if it would be possible to build two smaller niches in their place. She walked over to the alcove and examined it. As far as she could see, this side of the wall was newer than the rest of the house, and she recollected that the late Conde had had central heating installed in the Castelo. Obviously this outside wall had been broken for the purpose and no doubt the hot-water pipes ran through its length and were buried beneath the floor.

Still musing on the possibilities, her eyes ranged along a bookshelf, coming to rest on a leather-tooled volume. Without quite knowing why she picked it out and, opening it, was delighted to see it was the history of the Castelo. The thick pages were handprinted and the illustrations drawn delicately in ink and coloured with paint that still retained its luminosity. There was the drawing-room, almost identical to the present one, as well as the hall and the main *salon*. Only two rooms were different: the long gallery which had once housed the family portraits, and the library, which had had bookshelves lining all its walls. The alcove wall, as she had rightly assumed on seeing it, was of newer construction, and more than ever she was convinced that the room would be improved by taking away even more of the bookshelves and adding further niches.

Methodically she measured the room, wondering how deep she could make the alcoves. One foot, two feet? Again she picked up the book and leafed through the pages until she found the picture of the library as it had once been. According to the scale marked in the bottom corner, the room was eighteen feet. She frowned. That meant that the false wall was nearly three feet in depth. Wondering why such a large amount of space had been used to house a pipe that could not be more than a foot in diameter, she checked the measurements again. Perhaps there was a defect in the foundation of the Castelo and the outer wall had had to be reinforced? At all events, whatever it was, she must find out. If Carlos were here he could tell her, but as ever too impetuous to wait, Stephanie began to search for it herself. As far as she could tell the wall was composed of heavy plywood and as she tapped against it, it rang hollow. Curiosity stirred and she shifted some of the books. They were easily removable except for a large black leather volume at the bottom. She pulled sharply, but it was wedged tight and, annoyed that she had resorted to such childish inquisitiveness, she gave the book an angry thump. It revolved to the side and with surprise she saw a small knob on the wood behind. She ran her finger against it and felt it click out of position. Slowly the complete side of the bookcase shifted, and she peered through the narrow aperture disclosed.

It was too dark to see and, taking a cigarette-lighter from her handbag, she squeezed through. In the flickering glow she saw she was standing on the first step of a narrow stairway built between the thickness of the outer walls. Gingerly she climbed to the top and found herself facing a timbered door. Half expecting it to be locked, she turned the handle, surprised when it slid open noiselessly. The flame of her lighter spluttered and died out. Muttering, she flickered it into life again. The light was too dim for her to see, but she made out a switch on the wall and pressed it, drawing back with a gasp as a crystal chandelier blazed on.

With amazement she moved further into the room. It was obviously built over part of the library, and although only some ten feet square, held a large satinwood desk with inlaid mother-of-pearl. It was a beautiful piece of furniture and she walked over and ran her finger along the edge. The top of the table was loose and like a flap, lifted at her touch and swung open. She bent forward and peered inside. On a bed of black velvet were set out some few dozen articles: winking diamonds, a miniature portrait of a woman in a crinoline, a brooch of gold decorated with cloisonné enamel in translucent green and blue, and a complete parure – necklace, earrings, bracelet and tiara – of square-cut emeralds and rose diamonds. She closed the flap, wondering why these particular pieces were kept separate from the others: there was no doubt in her mind that they were part of the Collection. Even to her unknowledgeable eyes the articles here were every bit as precious as those in the long gallery.

Still puzzled, she walked to the door, pausing to look at a small mother-of-pearl cabinet fixed to the wall. One of the little doors was loose and as she walked past the motion of air trembled it open. She put out her hand to close it and as she did so, saw the sparkling jewel inside. Carefully she opened the cabinet and saw that it was the respository for the most magnificent pearl she had ever seen. Nearly two inches long, it was shaped like a pear and all round its outline were large multi-coloured diamonds, yellow, rose and blue-white. Reverently she held the jewel in her hand. In the light the pearl glistened like satin, palest pink with a hint of gold. She twisted it on her palm, drinking in its strange, exotic beauty.

"A giant tear," she thought, and even as the words were formed, felt horror seep through her. A tear! Of course, why hadn't she realized it before? In her palm she held the priceless Queen's Tear! The jewel which all the police in Europe were seeking.

CHAPTER EIGHT

WITHOUT realizing how she got upstairs again, Stephanie found herself in her bedroom. Her one thought was to leave the Castelo, but no matter how great the distance she put between herself and the library, the knowledge of her discovery would remain with her forever. So Johnny had been right after all! She was in no doubt that the jewellery she had seen in the turret room was stolen. This explained Carlos's anger when he had returned from abroad and found her in his home; why, when he had finally conceded to his mother's wish to redecorate the Castelo, he had been adamant at leaving the library untouched.

Sinking on the bed, she wondered what had made him change his mind. Perhaps he had become over-confident and believed no one would ever learn his secret? Dry-eyed, she stared around her. The heavy perfume of roses was wafted through the window on the slight breeze that rustled the edge of the leaves.

Carlos had so much: position, wealth and the tradition of an ancient lineage. It seemed incredible that he should be a thief.

She did not know how long she remained on the bed, but she must have dozed into an uneasy sleep, for when she woke again the sun was streaming through the window. Heavy-eyed, she washed, put on a fresh dress and still yawning, descended the stairs to the terrace. Her throat was dry and the aroma of coffee came pleasantly to her nostrils. Making her way to the breakfast-table in the corner, she was surprised to see the small, black-clad figure of the Condesa already seated there. It was rare for the old lady to be seen before lunchtime and Stephanie's expression was not lost on her.

"In this hot weather I find it difficult to sleep," the Condesa explained. "Besides, there is an atmosphere about the Castelo lately that is strange – almost as if something – something odd were about to happen."

"What sort of thing?" Stephanie asked the question as casually as she could.

"I don't know." The old lady poured herself some coffee. "Perhaps it is just my fancy. When we are old we get strange whims."

Silently Stephanie began her breakfast and it was not until she had almost finished that the Condesa spoke again.

"You're looking pale, my dear. I hope you don't find the heat too trying."

"I do a little. I'm not used to the sun in such large doses!"

"Well, your job here will soon be finished. My son mentioned to me last night that you will be leaving in a week or so."

"I'm leaving now." The words came out of their own volition, but as soon as they were spoken Stephanie realized she was going to act on them. Now that she knew the truth about the Marocs, nothing would induce her to stay. She closed her eyes, opening them again as the Condesa tapped her stick on the floor.

"You have certainly had too much sun. I have never seen you look so pale."

"I'm all right," Stephanie said quickly. "It's just – just that seeing my sister has made me homesick."

"In that case you should go back with her at once."

Instinctively Stephanie felt it was no sympathy at her homesickness that prompted the Condesa's remark. Yet what other reason could there be, unless the old lady knew what she had found in the library? She looked into the wrinkled face, but there was nothing to be read in the dark eyes that regarded her.

"I think perhaps you're right," she said slowly. "Felicity

hadn't planned to go home so soon, but I could go and stay at the inn with her. The Conde wanted me to stay on here, but—but—"

"There is no need to worry. I will make your excuses for you."

"Why don't you want me to tell him myself?" As soon as she had spoken Stephanie regretted the words. "I mean I—"

"I know what you mean. I merely think it best that you go without any farewells."

"I don't understand you."

"Don't you?" The Condesa leaned back in her chair and placed her cane carefully over the arm. "You have made yourself very likeable while you have been here, and I have appreciated your devoting your evenings reading to me. I know there are very few amusements here for a young woman."

"I came on business, not for amusement!"

"I know you did. But you are young and pretty and Carlos is aware of it."

The cup shook in Stephanie's hand and she placed it on the small table beside her. "You're talking in riddles, Condesa. I'd much rather you said exactly what's in your mind."

The old woman sighed. "It is difficult for me to tell you, but I will try. Carlos is a strange man. For years I have wanted him to marry, but since my husband died he has become less and less interested in women. It is as if he wants to play a—" She hesitated. "In America I think the expression is 'a lone hand'. And I do not like it. Carlos must marry and have sons." She paused. "Janique is the ideal wife for him."

"I'm sure she is." Stephanie's voice trembled. "But you flatter me if you suppose I could come between them."

"I don't intend to flatter you. But I know my son and I have seen the way he watches you."

"You're imagining things, Condesa."

"On the contrary. I know you haven't given him any

encouragement, but to a man like Carlos this is even more dangerous. Always women have run after him, but you, with your cool English ways, have persistently ignored him. I think," added the Condesa drily, "that he may well find the novelty irresistible."

Remembering the many times over the last few days when she had longed to throw herself into his arms, Stephanie gave a bitter smile.

"It is not a joke," the old lady rebuked. "For your own happiness you should go away."

"Is that your only reason?" Stephanie spoke softly. "Have you no other reason for wanting me to leave?"

The dark eyes did not waver. "That is my only reason. Because I am thinking of Carlos's future."

Stephanie did not reply. Everything the Condesa had said in this last surprising half-hour could have a double implication. Was she really afraid that Carlos was falling in love with an Englishwoman, or did she fear that she had discovered, or was on the brink of discovering, the turret room? Either way the question must remain unanswered, for Stephanie knew that having said all she had intended, the Condesa would say no more.

"You needn't worry." She got to her feet. "I intend leaving as soon as I can."

"I am glad. There are some things worth more than money."

"I know," Stephanie said quietly. "Peace of mind. You can never buy that."

Afraid that if she stayed any longer she would be unable to control her tears, she hurried out and, eyes lowered, did not see Carlos until he was almost on top of her. She stopped so suddenly that she would have fallen had he not put out his arms as a protection.

"You're always in a hurry. What's the rush this time?"

She murmured something and attempted to walk past, but he barred her way.

"I've been looking for you."

"What for?"

Dropping his arms from her shoulders, he reached in his pocket and drew out a small piece of rose-coloured velvet. "Janique found this in Lisbon. She thought it might be suitable for one of the walls in the main bedroom. Come, I'll show you."

"Can't it wait?"

"I would prefer that it didn't, unless you have something else you wish to do. You are seeing your sister, perhaps?"

"Not this morning. I'm meeting her later on."

"In that case you have no excuse."

Before she could find a suitable reply he walked ahead of her to the east wing. Trembling, she followed him and, looking at his dark head, the width of his shoulders, wished she were a million miles away.

At the far end of the corridor he flung open double doors leading into the main bedroom of the Castelo. Ornately decorated with heavy baroque furniture, it looked more suitable for a museum than a room in which to sleep. The four-poster bed stood on a dais, stiff rose-coloured hangings draped either side from gilt poles, while a gilt dressing-table and recamier were ranged by the window, which was also hung with the same, stiff rose material.

"What do you think of it?" he asked.

"Not to my taste," she answered bluntly.

"Nor mine either. But the room occupies the best position. Come and look at the view."

She followed him across the carpet and looked through the window at the sloping woodland. In the distance shimmered the blue sea, merging with the sky. A large balcony opened off the windows and Carlos stepped out on to it.

"I thought of putting garden furniture here and a breakfast-table, and some plants, perhaps."

"You're going to use this room?"

"Of course. It's the bridal suite."

Flushing, she turned away. "I see. Then perhaps you'll let me know your suggestions."

"By all means." He held out the piece of rose-coloured velvet he had shown her downstairs. "We thought of covering the walls in this material."

She took the velvet from him and walked back into the bedroom. "I wouldn't like it," she said slowly. "Velvet is too heavy for a bedroom – too stuffy. But then I like plenty of fresh air."

One black eyebrow lowered as Carlos looked at her. "I don't follow your reasoning. What has a wall to do with fresh air?"

"Velvet collects the dust," she replied. "Wallpaper would be much better."

"Ah. Now I understand."

"But that's only my opinion. This is your room – you'll have to sleep in it." She stopped, colouring slightly.

"There's no need to be embarrassed. It doesn't happen to be my room yet."

"It will be when you're married." As soon as the words were out she regretted them and turned away to examine the wall with more care than warranted.

"Of course I will use it when I'm married," he said softly. "All the Maroc heirs are born here." He closed the windows and moved to the centre of the room. "If you don't recommend the velvet we will have to think of something else."

"Please don't take my opinion," she said quickly. "You should ask Janique."

"I have asked you," he said quietly.

"I don't see why."

"Don't you?" As if her remark had inflamed him, he bridged the space between them and tilted her head so that she could not avoid looking at him. His hands were rough and strong, and she could not move away. "Look at me, Stephanie."

Knowing it was useless to disobey him, she raised her eyes to his. They were dark and serious, so close that she could see her reflection in their pupils.

"Why do you persist in baiting me?" he said huskily. "I've never met a girl who has treated me the way you do."

"Perhaps that is my attraction!"

"Don't talk in that fashion. It doesn't suit you to be sarcastic."

"I never pretend to be what I'm not."

"But you are a woman, and a woman should know when to give in."

"I would never give in to you, Carlos."

"You have made that plain enough." His voice grew harsh. "What is the matter with you, Stephanie? From the moment we met I knew there was an affinity between us. What has changed you lately?"

"After our conversation last night you've no right to talk to me like that."

"Forget what I said to you last night. When I am angry I will say anything that comes into my head. But when I am away from you I want you so desperately that—"

"Don't! I can't bear it!" She tried to pull away from him, but his grip tightened.

"Don't! Don't!" he grated. "That's all you can say to me. You are afraid of passion, Stephanie, afraid of allowing yourself to love."

"I'm not afraid!" she denied hotly. "But I don't want *you*. Can I make it plainer than that?"

"No, you can't."

Before she could stop him he pulled her into his arms, his body straining close and his mouth on hers vibrant with desire. For a moment she struggled against him and then, realizing it was useless, remained passive. Again and again he kissed her and in spite of herself, her pulses raced, the blood coursing through her veins ever more quickly and she felt herself responding to him. Her hands came up and clasped his head, stroking the dark hair. In an instant he was no longer in command of himself, no longer the arrogant master of the Castelo but a man with a pliant woman in his arms, a woman that he wanted.

Afraid of the passion she had evoked, she started to struggle again, but the gesture only inflamed him further and his mouth pressed heavier on hers.

"Carlos, don't! Let me go!" With a desperate effort she pushed him away and before he could stop her, twisted from his arms and ran out of the room. She sped down the corridor and up the stairs to the safety of her own bedroom. Locking the door, she sank down on the bed and rested her burning face in her hands. For a long while she remained immobile, then, standing up, walked over to the dressing-table and looked at her reflection in the mirror. Her mouth was bruised with Carlos's kisses, her eyes starry and brilliant with unshed tears.

"Oh God!" she cried. "What's going to happen to me? I love him, I love him."

She sank down on the dressing-stool and closed her eyes. How could one love and despise at the same time? Her anger towards Carlos rose sharply. His mother had said he was betrothed to Janique and yesterday he himself had practically confirmed it, yet he was still not averse to making love to another woman. Perhaps to a man like him conquest was of primary importance? She remembered all she had read of the Latin men: their impetuosity, their ardour, their ability to make love without loving. Lifting her head, she stared at her reflection again in the mirror and tried to divorce Carlos from his background, tried not to see him as a Portuguese aristocrat with a magnificent home. But it was impossible: his background had made him what he was and what he was, she loved.

"But I can't love a thief!" she told herself. In the turret room was jewellery worth thousands and thousands of pounds, jewellery he had bought knowing it had been stolen. "I can't love a thief!" she repeated. "I must get away before he finds out that I know."

A longing to confide in someone was so strong in her that she decided to go down to the village to talk to her sister. Always with Stephanie to think was to act, and before she could give herself a chance to change her mind, she was running down the drive.

The day was hot and sultry and she had only gone half a mile when she was streaming with perspiration, her hair damp and dark against her forehead. Her quick steps grew slower, her mood more despondent until finally she sank on to a boulder in the roadway to rest.

A motor-car chugged up the hill and she looked up, recognizing Johnny. As he drew level with her he stopped and she walked over and saw that her sister was sitting next to him.

"I was on my way down to see you," Stephanie said.

"Hop in." Felicity opened the door of the car. "What's the matter, darling? You look as if you've seen a ghost."

"I – nothing. It's too much sun."

Johnny glanced at her through the driving-mirror. "It's the first time since you've been here that the sun's affected you."

"I'm not lying," Stephanie retorted, "or do I have to say everything twice before you believe me?"

"Not at all. I just wondered if you might have any *other* reason for looking so distraught." He slowed the car and glanced round. "You wouldn't have discovered something at the Castelo, would you?"

"Of course not. I'd have told you if I had."

Johnny said no more, but his silence was significant and Stephanie knew he did not believe her. As though despairing of any further communication from her, he put his foot on the accelerator and soon drew up in front of the inn.

Together they walked into the hall and immediately a figure rose from an armchair and strode over to them.

"Hello, Robert—" Stephanie began, but stopped as he walked past her to Felicity.

"Where the hell do you think you've been?" he demanded.

Slowly Felicity looked up at him. "I beg your pardon?"

"I asked you where the hell you've been?"

"If you'd like to rephrase your question in a civilized manner I might consider answering it," she retorted, and turned a disdainful shoulder on him.

"Oh no, you don't, my girl!" He pulled her round to face him. "You needn't think I'm going to be put off by heavy sarcasm—"

"Will you please let go of me!" she demanded.

"Not until you've told me where you've been."

"Sightseeing with Johnny if you must know."

He dropped his hands from her shoulders. "Didn't it occur to you to tell me what your plans were instead of leaving me to kick my heels here all the morning?"

"I'm not your keeper," Felicity retorted, "and we don't have to pretend that we're lovebirds when we're on our own." She stalked upstairs and, seizing the opportunity to be alone with her sister, Stephanie followed.

As soon as the bedroom door closed behind them she recounted what had happened the night before: her restlessness, her decision to start work immediately on the library and her subsequent discovery of the turret room with its stolen treasures.

Felicity listened in horror. "That settles it. You can't possibly stay at the Castelo any longer. People like that are dangerous – you don't know what might happen."

"I've already told the Condesa I'm leaving. But I can't go until I've finished the library."

"For heaven's sake stop considering the job! It's your *safety* I'm worried about."

"They won't do anything to me."

"I wish I were so sure. People who steal will stop at nothing. If they think they might be discovered – and if everything you said about the jewels is true – there's a fortune at stake."

"But don't you see I've simply got to stay now? First I told Carlos I wouldn't and then I would. If I changed my mind again, he's bound to suspect something."

"I suppose so," Felicity said reluctantly. "But the thought

of you being there . . ." She frowned. "Why don't you tell Johnny?"

"I daren't. I couldn't bear it if he had Carlos—" Stephanie buried her head in her hands. "I'm so miserable I don't know what to do. By rights I should tell Johnny what I've learned, but when you love someone, everything else is unimportant."

"I know how you feel," Felicity said huskily. "But the fact still remains that Carlos is a thief – and I'm not going back to England and leave you here. You've simply got to finish the whole job in the next few days and come back with me."

"Very well." Stephanie looked up, the room blurring through her tears. "You've been wonderful about all this, Felicity. I can't thank you enough."

"Don't be so silly. Thanks aren't necessary between sisters. Now wipe your eyes and put on a smile – or else bulldog Johnny might become even more suspicious than he already is!"

Dressing for dinner that night Stephanie took great pains with her appearance. If all went well she would be leaving the Castelo in a few days and with feminine perversity she wanted Carlos to remember her looking her best. The dress she chose was one she had bought on a shopping trip in Lisbon. Of palest pink organza, it floated round her like a cloud, from which rose the curve of gleaming shoulders and graceful neck. She had never before worn pink, but she was glad now that she had listened to the advice of the saleswoman, for the subtle colour was reflected in deeper tones by her Titian hair. She looked very young, her eyes large and brilliant with emotion as she walked through the main *salon* and down the wide sweeping stairs, her footsteps echoing through the picture-lined room.

The drawing-room was empty, but from the terrace came the subdued murmur of voices and the clink of ice in glasses. Only a few shaded lamps had been switched on and through the wide windows glimmered the starry Portuguese night. For a moment she remained immobile and as she moved, the tall figure of a man stepped through the open window.

It was Carlos, a Carlos she had never seen before. His white shirt front was slashed by a wide blue ribbon bearing the insignia of some noble order, and a jewelled cross was pinned to the breast of his evening jacket.

He was the first to break the silence. "I'm sorry if I frightened you this afternoon, Stephanie. You must know I wouldn't hurt you for the world."

She half turned her head away. "You had no right to kiss me."

"Must there be a right before a man takes a woman in his arms?"

Without answering she stepped back. Her skirt brushed the lamp behind her and it toppled. With an exclamation Carlos reached out to catch it before it fell and then held it aloft so that it shed its light over her as she stood in front of him.

"How beautiful you look," he said quietly. "But how cold you are – and strange."

She laughed shortly. "*I'm* not the one who's strange."

He continued to stare at her, his eyes grave, his mouth set. "If my behaviour appears odd at times, there is a reason for it. Stephanie, I must talk to you."

"You're always talking to me."

He shook his head. "Don't deliberately misunderstand me, *cara*. You know what I mean. I want to talk to you without quarrelling – logically."

Logically! The word pointed the way for her actions. The only logical course was to tell him that she knew he was a thief and then to leave the Castelo. She clenched her hands.

"Stephanie, please, please come with me."

"No, Carlos. We've nothing to say to each other."

"But you can't go on being annoyed with me because I lost my temper the other night. I'm always losing my temper, and you must forgive me."

"I forgave you a long time ago, but I don't see that there is any necessity for us to talk to each other any more."

"You are still angry with me because of what I said about Janique."

"I don't give a damm about Janique!" Stephanie said fiercely. "For God's sake, Carlos, you can't expect me to pretend that I care what you do with your life!"

"*Mae de Deus!*" His voice was full of fury. "How dare you talk to me like this? I have bowed down before you. I have humbled myself as a Maroc has never before humbled himself to a woman, yet you have a heart of stone. How can you stand there and pretend you don't know what I'm trying to tell you? How can you go on throwing at me the things that you drove me into saying?"

"Carlos, stop it!"

"I won't. From the moment I saw your eyes blazing at me with anger, and your red hair glowing like fire, I knew you were the only woman for me." He took her hands and pulled her close. "You are my jewel," he whispered. "*Cara, cara.*"

"No! I don't want to hear any more!" Desperately she pulled away from him and ran on to the terrace, glad that the swinging lanterns suspended from the trees did not fully illumine her face.

Janique, resplendent in gold brocade, was deferentially talking to the Condesa in her inevitable black and standing to one side was Miguel, sipping a glass of champagne, also in evening dress, across his breast a narrower ribbon with a smaller jewelled cross.

"You're only just in time for a drink, Stephanie," he said, raising his glass to her. "We're leaving for Lisbon in a few minutes."

"Lisbon?"

"Didn't you know? The Duque de Corbesco is giving a party and we've all been invited. I thought my mother had mentioned it to you this afternoon."

"I'm afraid I forgot," the Condesa said, and even as she

spoke Stephanie knew that she was lying and that the omission had been a deliberate one.

"Even if I'd known about it," Stephanie said quietly, "I wouldn't have been able to come."

"Why not?" Carlos spoke directly behind her and she swung round, her filmy skirts brushing his leg.

"I have a headache. I felt it coming on all day."

His glance travelled from her shining hair to her gold sandals and back again to her face. Steadily he looked into her eyes, his expression telling her as plainly as words that he did not believe her excuse. Still in silence he moved to the table and poured champagne into crystal goblets.

"A toast," he said, handing the glasses round. "To the future – may it be happier than the past."

A thin breeze stirred the branches and the lanterns swung, casting pointed shadows on the terrace. Stephanie, standing a little apart, watched the scene as if it were a tableau: the two dark men, the tiny shrivelled Condesa and the glinting, golden Janique.

They drank the toast and under cover of the general conversation Carlos returned to Stephanie's side, half shielding her with his body as he spoke.

"You offered a poor excuse just now. You would have enjoyed yourself at the party. The Duque is renowned for them."

"No doubt he is. But being English, I'm afraid I wouldn't fit into Portuguese society."

"I'm the best judge of that. And Janique isn't entirely Portuguese either – her father is French."

"Nevertheless, this is her sort of life. It isn't mine."

"You are very blunt," he said coldly.

"Only because you have shown me that you don't understand anything other than plain speaking."

He said nothing and she clasped her hands together, shivering slightly. "I am leaving the Castelo in a few days, Carlos. There will be no need for me to stay any longer."

"You can't leave yet." His face was bleak, his voice dry. "I give you my promise that I will not bother you any more with unwelcome attentions."

"I tell you, I can't stay."

His eyes flashed. "Are you doubting my word?"

Before he could reply, Janique came towards them.

"We must be going, Carlos. It is late." The girl looked at Stephanie, her dark eyes mocking. "I can see you are dressed up for an occasion, Miss North. Are you expecting someone?"

"No."

Janique shrugged and, having made her point, put her hand through Carlos's arm. Instantly he bent towards her, suave and in control of himself.

"I am ready now, my dear," he said, and for the first time in Stephanie's presence lapsed into Portuguese.

Listening to the lilting language, Stephanie felt more than ever alien and moved across to the terrace to lean against the balustrade. Bleakly she watched the family drive away and only when the tail-light of Carlos's Mercédès and Miguel's sports car could be seen no more, did she sink on to one of the hammocks and close her eyes. Backwards and forwards she swung, the only sound being the creaking of the springs and the chirping of the cicadas. Her eyes closed and gradually the noises receded as she fell asleep.

She awoke with the feeling that she was no longer alone and, sitting up, her heart started to thump as she saw the slim, fair-haired man perched opposite her.

"Johnny! What are you doing here?"

"I came to talk to you." He grinned lightheartedly, but she sensed the threat behind the words.

"I told you this afternoon that I had nothing to say."

"I know you did, my dear, but I don't happen to believe you."

"I can't help that," she said sharply. "I'm leaving the Castelo very soon, Johnny. You'll have to get your information without me."

"Why the sudden haste to depart?"

"There's nothing sudden about it. I've nearly finished my work."

"Is that so? You didn't seem in any hurry before though." Johnny came across and sat next to her. The hammock swung beneath his weight and with one foot he pushed it back and forth. "You're looking very glamorous, my dear. You should always wear pink."

"Thank you," she said drily. "But compliments will get you nowhere."

His laugh was sudden. "You're in a very sharp mood tonight. I can see your nerves are on edge." He took out a cigarette and carefully lit it, flinging the match into a flower-filled urn beside him.

"You don't happen to have a pin, do you?" he said conversationally.

"I'm afraid not. Why?"

"Because you look as if you're sitting on one. Relax, my dear, and tell me what you've discovered."

"I haven't discovered anything."

Johnny stopped swinging the hammock and his slight body tensed as he hunched himself forward. "You're not telling me the truth! The look of fear when you opened your eyes and saw me was too much of a giveaway. You've found something and I want to know what it is."

"I haven't found anything I tell you – I'm not your spy!"

"Would you rather be an accomplice to a thief?"

"How dare you!" Her hand reached out to strike him but he caught it in mid-air, his grip hard as steel.

"Don't be silly," he said quietly. "I don't want to offend you, but neither am I going to let you fob me off with a pack of lies. This is a serious business, Stephanie, and I'm convinced I've come to the end of my search here. If you won't help me, I'm going to get in touch with Interpol. They'll set the police in Lisbon on Maroc's track."

"You can't do that! Carlos may be innocent."

"Then he won't have anything to worry about when we search the Castelo." Johnny looked at her grimly. "If I'd thought you were telling me the truth a moment ago, I'd know now that you weren't. A child would know you're hiding something." Stephanie did not answer and he heaved a sigh. "Ah well," he said, drawing on his cigarette, "with a search warrant of my own I needn't rely on you. I'm disappointed in you, Stephanie, I thought you were on my side."

"I don't want to be on anybody's side, I tell you. Leave me alone!"

"Very well, my dear, I will. I'll go now – but I'll be back."

Vaulting over the balustrade he dropped on to the lawn; she heard the pad of his footsteps and then there was silence. Trembling, she got up and leaned her elbows on the balustrade, trying to think clearly. Within hours, a day at most, Johnny would return with the police. Even if they didn't believe him, once he laid all his evidence before them, and with pressure from Interpol, they would have to search the Castelo. As easily as she had discovered the turret room, there was no question but that Johnny too would find it. He might look bland and easy-going, but she was in no doubt as to his capabilities and perception.

She visualized the police climbing the narrow stairs and entering the turret room. She could see them lifting the lid of the desk and opening the small doors of the cabinet on the wall. "I can't let it happen!" she thought. "I can't!" She paced the terrace, her skirts whirling in a pink arc, her flying thoughts keeping pace with her steps.

Later that night, slumped exhaustedly in an armchair in her own room, Stephanie heard the family return. Janique's voice floated up to her above the heavier tones of Carlos and his laugh, deep and untroubled. Her hands clenched at her side and she wondered for the thousandth time why she should bother to protect him. How could you love a man you despised? How indeed could you love a man you hardly knew? "It isn't love," she said to herself. "It's physical attraction. It's his maleness and arrogance that appeal to me. The real Carlos is someone I loathe."

She repeated these words to herself as she stood by her

bedroom door and waited for the family to retire. Since her stay at the Castelo she had noticed that Miguel was nearly always the last to go to his room. Apparently devoted to music, he would lock himself in the library and listen to gramophone records for hours, and there had been many occasions when far into the night she had heard the strains of Beethoven and Bach echoing along the gallery. Tonight again there was the sound of music, and she hurried downstairs. The electric lights had been switched off, but at widely spaced intervals on the walls candles spluttered their final flickering light. The hall was nearly dark as she tapped at the library door. There was no answer and she tapped again more loudly.

"Who is it?" Miguel called.

"It's me – Stephanie."

Footsteps sounded and a key was turned in the lock. The door opened and Miguel stepped out. "I thought you were in bed long ago. Is anything wrong?"

"I've got to talk to you."

"My dear girl," he said softly, "you're as pale as a ghost." He put his hand on her shoulder and she shivered. "You're trembling!"

"Am I?" she said dully. "For the past few hours I don't know what I've been doing."

Without answering he pulled her into the library. The curtains had been drawn and the electric fire switched on to ward off the evening chill. Quickly he poured a brandy and handed it to her. Gratefully she sipped and after a moment stopped trembling.

"I feel better now, thanks."

"You look it, too. In fact I've never seen you look lovelier." She did not answer and he smiled. "You don't like me complimenting you, perhaps?"

"I haven't time for compliments."

"You had more time for me before my brother came on the scene."

"Carlos has nothing to do with it."

"I'm afraid he has. That's why I stepped out of the picture and left you to him."

"I don't want to be left for anybody, thank you. I'm not a statue."

He laughed. "I wish you were. Then I could place you on a pedestal and look at you whenever I liked." His voice lowered to a caress. "You look as if you were made of pink alabaster. I've never seen such pearly skin."

Exasperated, Stephanie stood up. The last thing she wanted was to flirt with Miguel. "Please be serious," she pleaded. "I've got to talk to you about something important. You're a member of the family and . . ." She paused. "I don't know how to tell you this, but I – I know all about the library."

"Indeed? What do you know about it?"

She leaned forward. "I know about the turret room."

"*Mae de Deus!*" Miguel tensed in his chair. "So you've found out, have you?" He put his hand in his pocket and slowly stood up. "What are you going to do?"

"I don't know. For the past two hours I've done nothing but think about it." She told him all that had happened since she had found the turret room and learned of Johnny's identity. "We must do something Miguel," she finished urgently. "The police will be here in a few hours. We've got to protect Carlos!"

A strange expression crossed Miguel's face and he took his hand from his pocket and placed it on her shoulder. "So you want to protect Carlos?" he said softly. "That's extremely kind of you, Stephanie. I never realized until now how sympathetic you were."

"*Please*, Miguel," she said desperately. "We haven't time for compliments. We must do something *now*."

"Of course. We'll have to empty the turret room and hide the jewels somewhere until the police have gone." He turned to the door. "I'll tell Carlos."

"Is that wise?"

He turned round and looked at her. "That's a good question," he said at last. "I'm not sure it *would* be wise. If I could do it myself . . ."

"Why can't you?" she said eagerly. "You could hide the stuff where Carlos won't find it, and then afterwards you could return it."

"Return it!" Anger distorted his expression. "You must be mad! Those jewels can never be returned now – never, I tell you."

"But they're stolen. How *can* you keep them?"

For a long moment Miguel did not answer, then his shoulders bowed and he sank down on a chair. "I've got to protect the family name, Stephanie. Ever since I found Carlos was buying this stolen jewellery I've pleaded with him to stop. But he wouldn't – once he makes up his mind nothing can make him alter it. But whatever he is, he's still my brother. He's still the Conde de Maroc." He looked up and even from a distance Stephanie saw the glitter of moisture in his eyes. "I've got to protect Carlos and you must help me. Don't breathe a word to *anyone* about this."

"Do you think I could?" she said bitterly. "If I'd had any sense I'd have told Johnny already."

"You wouldn't dare!" He sprang up and caught her violently by the arms. "You wouldn't dare, Stephanie!"

She closed her eyes to hide the sudden uprush of tears. "No," she said huskily. "Carlos's secret is safe with me."

"You don't know how relieved I am to hear you say that! Now go to your room. I promise I'll do what I can. Mr. Carlton will find nothing incriminating when he arrives here."

CHAPTER NINE

STEPHANIE slept little that night and when she did her dreams were filled with strange shadowy figures. As soon as it was daylight she dressed and slipped down the stairs. In the cool light of morning she wondered whether she had done the right thing in telling Miguel of Johnny's true identity. After all, he had told her who he was in confidence and she should have kept his secret.

'But I didn't want him to confide in me,' she argued with herself. 'I don't owe him any more loyalty than I owe – Carlos.'

In any case, the matter was out of her hands and there was nothing she could do about it. Feeling that she must confide in someone, she went to the telephone and dialled the number of the inn.

Felicity had just finished dressing when she was called to the phone and with growing horror listened to Stephanie's recital of the previous day's events. When she learned her sister had disclosed Johnny's identity to Miguel de Maroc, she could contain herself no longer.

"You must be out of your mind!" she exclaimed. "Don't you realize the danger you've put yourself in?"

"Don't be silly," Stephanie said angrily. "You're making a melodrama of it."

"I'm not making it out any worse than it is. For heaven's sake pack your things and come down here right away."

But Stephanie's only answer was to put down the phone, and Felicity shook her head and walked slowly back to her room.

Her first instinct was to confide in Robert and realizing it was no good waiting till they were at breakfast – for almost certainly Johnny would be there – she crossed the hall and tapped on Robert's door.

Razor in hand, he turned round from the mirror as she came in, and listened with growing horror as Felicity repeated what her sister had told her.

"I don't see why the future of the Marocs should be any concern of hers," he said finally. "The man's a crook and deserves to pay the penalty."

"Stephanie loves Carlos," Felicity told him quietly. "You can't expect her to run away and leave him to face imprisonment."

Robert tossed his towel into the basin and sank on to a chair. "I suspected it was something like this the moment I saw the two of them together. The best thing she can do is to go back to England as soon as possible. Once she's home she'll forget all about him."

"I'm not so sure of that," Felicity replied slowly. "It will take her a long time to get over Carlos."

Robert picked up a hairbrush from the dressing-table and smoothed his hair down. "Women forget. Nobody goes on being in love for ever."

"I wish I could agree with you." Tears muffled Felicity's voice and Robert swung round in surprise.

"My dear girl, whatever's the matter with you?"

She did not answer and clumsily he pulled her into his arms. But his attempt at comfort only seemed to intensify her sobs.

"It's Johnny, isn't it?" he asked huskily. "I'm so sorry, my dear."

Marvelling that a man could be so blind, Felicity pulled away from his arms. "I'm sorry to make such a fool of myself. I've never cried in front of you before, Robert."

"Don't apologize," he said quietly. "It's the first time I've seen you so human. As a matter of fact, it wasn't until we came to Portugal that I . . ."

His voice trailed away and though Felicity looked at him hopefully, he said nothing further.

With a sigh she walked to the door. "I'm going to phone Stephanie again and tell her she's got to come back with us. We'll go as soon as we can get seats on the plane."

"I'll see about altering our reservations right away." Robert came across and looked down at her, his blunt face serious and troubled. "If there's anything I can do to help you with Johnny . . ."

"No!" Not trusting herself to say any more, Felicity ran out of the room and Robert stared after her.

What an idiot Johnny Carlton was. Couldn't he see what a lovely girl Felicity was? Swearing beneath his breath, he slipped on his jacket and went down to breakfast.

After her conversation with Felicity, Stephanie did not feel like eating any breakfast, but she wandered on to the terrace and helped herself to some coffee. She had just poured a second cup when Miguel appeared and crossed the terrace towards her.

"I've been waiting to see you," she said rapidly. "Have you managed to empty the turret room yet?"

"No. Carlos stayed in the library for most of last night and I did not have any opportunity. But don't worry, everything will be moved out of there today."

With this promise Stephanie had to be content, but her anxiety did not abate and she wandered restlessly about the Castelo, doing her best to avoid Carlos, and every now and then peering through the window to see if Johnny had returned. It was not until early evening that she saw with relief Carlos and Janique drive away, and immediately she went down to the library. But there was no sign of Miguel and though she waited in the hall, she did not see him until the gong sounded for dinner.

The Condesa was already in the dining-room when she arrived and she had to sit through the meal without the chance of a word alone with him. He seemed his normal suave self and although she tried to catch his eyes in the hope of reading some reassuring message in them, she failed to do so.

At last dessert was finished and the Condesa led the way to the drawing-room. Under cover of taking her coffee cup from Miguel, she was able to ask him if he had cleared the turret room, and was dismayed when he shook his head. But she had no chance to question him further, for he moved over to the settee and sat next to his mother.

At ten o'clock the Condesa rose and retired to her room and as soon as the door closed behind her, Stephanie turned to Miguel.

"Let me help you empty the room," she said urgently. "We've got no time to lose."

"That won't be necessary," he replied. "This is something that I've got to do alone. Now go to bed like a good girl and leave the job to me."

Realizing the futility of arguing with him, Stephanie did as she was told, but she was too restless to go to bed and nervously paced the room. One hour went by, two hours, and although nearly dropping with fatigue, she could not settle down to sleep.

Suddenly she heard the sound of a motor purring along the drive and running to the window, saw the Mercédès draw up and Carlos help Janique out. They disappeared into the house and she heard their footsteps on the stairs and then Carlos's deep voice and Janique's answering laugh.

Stephanie sat on the edge of the bed and rested her head against one of the posts. She would give them half an hour to retire and then she would go downstairs and see what Miguel was doing. She lowered her head to the pillow and closed her eyes. How tired she was, how exhausted . . .

When she awoke again the pale light of dawn was seeping through the room and with a start she realized she had fallen into a deep sleep. Angry with herself, she ran stealthily along the corridor and down the stairs to the library.

The room was deserted and her glance went to the bookcase covering the secret door. Surely by now Miguel had hidden the jewels! Holding her lighter aloft, she climbed the turret stairs and pressed the switch. Momentarily dazzled by the bright light she stepped back and as she did so, stumbled over a figure on the floor. A scream rose to her lips, dying away as she recognized Miguel. He was lying on his back, his arms flung out, his eyes closed. She bent to loosen his collar.

Her glance flew to the open bureau and then to the cabinet which housed the Queen's Tear. Both pieces of furniture were empty!

Desperately she tried to bring Miguel back to consciousness and was about to go down to the library in search of brandy when he stirred and opened his eyes.

"Where am I?" he muttered thickly. "What happened?"

"You must have fainted," she answered. "Lie still and I'll get some water."

"No, I'm all right." He struggled to his feet and, swaying, leaned against the wall. "If only you'd come sooner," he gasped. "It's too late now, Carlos came up and found me here."

"You don't mean he's taken the jewels?"

Miguel nodded, the movement of his head causing him to sway. "I tried to stop him, but . . ." He put his hand to his jaw. "It was hopeless. He's much stronger than I am."

Anger welled in Stephanie. So Carlos had outwitted them after all! How had he discovered his brother was going to take the jewels away from the turret room? She pondered the question as she helped Miguel down the stairs and into the library, a frown still on her face as she poured some brandy from the decanter.

"Drink this, then you'll feel better."

He took the glass and drained it. The alcohol brought colour to his face and after a moment he was able to talk again. "It was cursed bad luck Carlos should take it into his head to come up to the turret room before he went to bed. As soon as he saw me with the suitcase he guessed what I was doing." His expression grew ugly. "I'll find out where he's put those jewels if it's the last thing I do."

"It could very *easily* be the last thing you'll do," a deep voice said behind them, and Stephanie swung round to see Carlos watching them.

His eyes travelled over her and she shrank back slightly, conscious that beneath her silk dressing-gown she was wearing nothing but a chiffon nightdress. The folds of amethyst material clung to her soft figure, revealing every curve, and nervously she clutched them closer, pushing back the soft red hair that fell in disorder to her shoulders.

"I never expected to see *you* here, Stephanie," Carlos said quietly. "But as you seem to know all about our infamous collection, perhaps you'd be good enough to tell me with whom else you share your knowledge – apart from my brother Miguel?"

She flushed. "I haven't said a word to anyone. I wasn't going to tell Miguel either until I learned that Johnny—"

"Ah!" Carlos's hands were heavy on her shoulders and he swung her around to face him. "So Mr. Carlton isn't the innocent tourist he would have me believe! I should have guessed as much when I found him skulking in the grounds. Exactly how does he come into this?"

"He's a detective . . ." In halting sentences Stephanie told him of her discovery of the turret room and its priceless contents, of Johnny Carlton's identity and his warning that he would be returning to the Castelo with a search warrant.

"That's why I went to Miguel," she concluded. "He promised to help you. After all, he's your brother and whatever you feel about each other he wouldn't want you to be caught."

"Caught!" Carlos spat out the word, his face so pale that his eyes blazed dark. "You've a very high opinion of me, haven't you, Stephanie? Last night you accused me of being a libertine. Today I am a thief. If you—"

The rest of his words were drowned by the screech of brakes and with an exclamation he pulled aside the curtain

153

and looked through the window. "It's Carlton," he said. "He's got some men with him. You'd better go into the dining-room, Miguel. You're in no state to be seen by the police."

Miguel staggered to his feet and in one stride Carlos was by his side, helping him from the room.

Almost immediately knocking reverberated through the hall. The slow footsteps of Dinis crossed the floor and heavy bolts were drawn. The door swung open and Johnny Carlton pushed his way in, stopping as he saw Stephanie on the threshold of the library.

"I see you were expecting me," he said quietly.

"Naturally. You said you would be here." She tried to smile. "I anticipated your bringing half the Lisbon police force."

"I have two men with me and more stationed in the grounds, although I hope it won't be necessary to call them. I've also got a search warrant which I intend to use."

"By all means," she replied. "But I can promise you, you won't find anything in the Castelo."

Johnny's eyes narrowed. "The biggest mistake I ever made was in trying to enlist your aid. I never thought you'd rat on me."

She turned scarlet. "That's a cruel thing to say! I don't owe you any more loyalty than – than I do Carlos."

"I shouldn't think a thief deserves any loyalty! That's why I asked you to help me."

She turned her back on him. "You have your search warrant. You don't need my help *now*."

For a moment he remained undecided, then he walked into the library. "I might as well start here. I'm pretty sure there's a secret passage somewhere in the Castelo." He looked at her keenly. "It would save time if you could tell me where it is. Or would that be disloyal too?"

"Certainly not. I've no objection to showing you."

This was the last reply he expected and he watched as she walked over to the bookcase and pressed the large black volume with her hand. The panel swung back and seeing the stairs behind, Johnny disappeared inside.

Stephanie sat down and wished miserably that she were miles away from Portugal, that she had never come to the Castelo and met Carlos. Johnny had every right to be angry with her. By her action she had thwarted him at the very moment when he had been so near his goal. Aiding a thief? No fine words could disguise the fact. Tears filled her eyes and she sniffed miserably.

A sound at the door made her turn and Carlos came in, his glance going to the open bookcase.

She answered his unspoken question. "Johnny's in the turret room with a search warrant."

"I see." He came over and sat down on the settee. They were close together, yet separated by a force she did not understand. She longed to talk to him, but words would not come out and she waited in silence, relieved as she heard footsteps on the stairs and Johnny came down. His face was pale and angry, his mouth set in a narrow line.

"You've been very clever, Conde," he said, "but you won't get the better of me. I know you're the thief and I'll pin it on you if it takes me the rest of my life. I'd have got you this time if it hadn't been for *her!*" He flung a look of fury at Stephanie and, intercepting it, Carlos stood up.

"You mustn't blame anyone, Mr. Carlton. You must only blame yourself for not keeping your own counsel." He walked over to the desk and opening a silver cigarette-box, held it out. When no one accepted, he took a cigarette himself and lit it, each action calm and deliberate. "When I learned of your impending arrival I was forced into precipitate action. You may look as long as you want, but you will never find the jewels. And because I know this I am going to tell you the truth. For a long time I have kept silent, but now there is nothing to be gained by it. I don't blame you for being bitter, Mr. Carlton. Neither can I blame you for thinking me a thief. However, there is something I would like you to know."

"I don't want to hear," Johnny said furiously.

155

"I'm afraid you must. I won't keep you long." There was so much command in his words that Johnny subsided. Only then did Carlos speak, his voice so low that it was barely audible in the still room.

"I'm not a thief," he began, "although I wish I could claim the same for the rest of my family."

Speaking with difficulty, as if each word caused him pain, he told them the story of the Maroc Collection and, listening to it, Stephanie was amazed at the way the facts fell clearly into position. The late Conde de Maroc had stopped at nothing to acquire what he wanted, and his whole life had been devoted not only to building up the Collection on view in the long gallery, but also to collecting the fabulous jewels he had hidden in the turret room. Neither Carlos nor Miguel had known of their father's obsession until after his death, when he had left them a letter revealing the whereabouts of his collection of stolen treasures.

"You will appreciate," Carlos said, "that it was a shock to us when we discovered that our father . . ." He paused. "I was determined that every piece of stolen jewellery should be restored to its original owners, but unfortunately Miguel did not agree with me. Not only was he determined to keep everything in the turret room, but he did his best to add to it. That explains his trips abroad. Always he was on the track of a new piece and sometimes he managed to buy it before I could stop him. It hasn't been an easy task for me, as you can imagine."

"Why couldn't you have returned the jewellery to the police?" Johnny asked. "That would have solved everything."

"It would also have brought disgrace to our name, and that I am determined never to do. So far I have sent half the stuff back to its rightful owners, but I can assure you that every piece will be returned even if it takes the rest of my life to do it!"

He stopped speaking and the only sound in the room was the faint ticking of the ormolu clock on the bureau. Stephanie blinked the tears away, marvelling that she could ever have been so blind as to misjudge Carlos.

"I don't know what to say," she whispered.

"There is *nothing* to say," he replied. "The very fact of your doubting me tells me you don't know me as well as I know you."

"But *I* know you." Johnny's sharp voice broke across the words as he turned to Stephanie. "We two are the only people who know the full story. You've got to come to London with me and corroborate what I tell my employers."

"I can't, Johnny!"

"You must. Although I know the jewels were here, you're the only one who's actually *seen* them. Without you, they won't believe me."

"I can't, I tell you! You mustn't ask me. You won't find the jewels again. I don't see how it will help if I come back with you."

"I *will* find them," Johnny said confidently, and looked at Carlos. "You don't think I'm going to let the matter rest here, do you?"

"I know you won't," the Portuguese replied. "But the jewels will be returned before you can find them again. Don't have any hard feelings against Stephanie. As my wife it would be impossible for her to do as you wish."

"Your wife!" Johnny exclaimed.

"Yes. Miss North and I became engaged yesterday."

Johnny got to his feet and the two men faced one another, the dark saturnine countenance of Carlos staring implacably into the ascetic, fair-skinned one. Stephanie held her breath and waited, praying desperately that Johnny would let the matter rest.

"Even if I take your word that you'll return the jewels," the Englishman said slowly, "I've still got to make my report. I've wasted two years of my time on this case, Conde. You must appreciate it makes me bitter."

"I wish we could have met under other circumstances," Carlos said.

"So do I. As it is, you seem to have won."

Without another word Johnny turned on his heel and a moment later Stephanie saw the car drive slowly out of sight.

Now that she was alone with Carlos she knew a sudden embarrassment and remained staring fixedly out of the window. She heard him move closer behind her and then felt his arms pulling her back to rest against him. For a moment she relaxed but, feeling the insidious warmth of his body, she pulled away.

"Why did you say that? You had no right . . ."

"I had every right. I love you, Stephanie."

"You can't love me. You've never told me so before."

"Because I didn't want to frighten you."

"I don't believe you." She tried to move away from him. "We've got to talk first."

"We've all our lives in which to talk," he murmured. "Be still and let me love you."

"No," she said again, and pushed her hands against his chest. "Don't make me fight you, Carlos. You're stronger than me and you'll win, but it will only be a physical battle."

"So," he said with a smile. "And you think that wouldn't satisfy me?"

"Not for long," she said shakily. "You wouldn't want a wife who hated you."

The words stung him and he dropped his hands to his sides. "You're right," he said. "I would never take an unwilling woman. But I don't believe you *are* unwilling. That's why I announced our engagement to Mr. Carlton. It was the only way I could make him stop pestering you."

"But there was no need to be quite so gallant," she said coldly. "I'm perfectly able to take care of myself."

"That's a great pity," he replied. "I was hoping you'd let me do it for the rest of our lives. I love you and I believe you love me. So many things I found inexplicable about your behaviour have now fallen into place. I can see why you were fighting me all the time. You thought I was a thief, didn't you?" She did not answer and he went on: "That was the only reason, wasn't it, Stephanie? If it hadn't been for that you'd have given in to me a long while ago. I know you love me."

"I don't!" Once again Stephanie lied, for even though she knew Carlos was innocent, she still believed they could have no future together. Every word that the Condesa had said had burnt itself indelibly into her brain. They were a man and woman of different races with a different background and tradition and they could never make a successful marriage.

"Why are you lying to me?" he asked huskily. "Even when you thought I was a thief you still did all you could to help me. You even lied to your own countryman." His eyes were dark and smouldering. "I can't believe you would do that unless you cared for me. There's a reason why you are still fighting me, Stephanie, and I'm not going to let you leave this room until I know what it is. Be honest with me, *cara mia*. We've seen too much of reality to be anything else."

Stephanie raised her head, and looking into the tanned face so near her own, knew it was impossible to lie any more. Subterfuge was a weak and childish thing, a game indulged in during the carefree months of courtship; yet she and Carlos had had no courtship: from antagonism they had crossed straight into love.

"You're right, Carlos," she said at last. "I do love you – almost from the first moment we met. But I can't marry you." She put her hand against his chest to prevent him pulling her close. "No, you must let me talk first, and I can't talk while you are holding me."

"Very well." He stepped away from her and sat down on the edge of the settee. "I am prepared to hear you out."

"We're too different," she said haltingly, "and you once said that people of different nationalities could never come together."

"My dear, you're misquoting me. I said that only a great love could surmount the barrier of different races. But I know that *my* love is great enough if yours can equal it."

"You think so at the moment, but you might not feel the same in a few years' time. You want me because I am the first woman that has opposed you. All the others have fallen into your lap."

A glint came into his eyes and he moved farther back on the settee and crossed one leg over the other. He looked nonchalant and at ease, yet watching him, she sensed the hidden power, the dominance that made him so much the arrogant master of the Castelo.

"Are you suggesting," he asked genially, "that if you had fallen into my lap, I would no longer have wanted you?"

"Yes."

He smiled ironically. "How little you know your man, *cara*. I will admit that I was attracted to you at first because you were different from other women. But I do not love you because you fought me but because you are beautiful and intelligent with a great deal of spirit and courage. All these things will remain yours even though you become submissive to my will."

She lifted her head, her eyes flashing. "I would never be submissive to you or any man!"

"In that case," he replied, getting to his feet, "we will have to go on fighting – but in a very nice way, of course."

"Carlos, you're making a joke of what I'm saying!"

"But naturally. You don't expect me to take you seriously? I love you, Stephanie. When are you going to get that into your stupid head? I want to marry you. I wouldn't care if you come from Timbuctoo but I intend to make you the mistress of the Castelo!"

Gently he pulled her into his arms and as his mouth found hers, Stephanie knew that she had come home at last. He had kissed her many times before, but this was the first kiss of declared love. Stroking the heavy eyebrows and the line of his arrogant nose, she knew she never wanted to leave his side.

"Kiss me," he breathed. "Kiss me back, my red-headed little devil!"

Stephanie raised her mouth, her lips parting as she responded to his passion, her only desire to give him everything she possessed.

"Forgive me for interrupting you," a shrill voice said. "Is this charming exhibition put on for my benefit?"

Stephanie pulled away from Carlos's arms, colour mounting to her cheeks as she saw Janique. She felt Carlos stiffen, saw his face pale as he moved towards the French girl.

"Janique my dear, I'm sorry you should have come in and seen us like this."

"I'm sure you are." The voice was mocking. "It's a good thing I don't object to a little flirtation." She turned to Stephanie. "But now I feel you've outstayed your welcome. It's time you returned to England, Miss North."

"You don't understand," Carlos said sharply. "Stephanie has promised to become my wife."

Looking at Janique's pale face, Stephanie felt unexpected sympathy. With a supreme effort the girl pulled herself together, forcing a smile to her lips as she held out her hand.

"I never realized the English were such fast workers," she murmured. "Allow me to congratulate you."

Embarrassed at the barely disguised venom, Stephanie was reluctant to take the hand held out to her, but feeling it would be churlish to refuse, she did so, murmuring her thanks and moving closer to Carlos's side.

"It's been a shock to me too," she said hesitantly. "Carlos – Carlos only proposed a little while ago."

"So I gathered." Janique's eyes narrowed. "If I'd known his affections were engaged elsewhere I'd have saved myself a trip."

Marvelling at Janique's honesty, Stephanie knew that had the positions been reversed she would never have had the courage to admit the truth. As if sensing what Stephanie felt, Janique sauntered over to the settee and, taking out a handkerchief, delicately wiped her eyes.

"Your mother is anxious to see you, Carlos. That's why I came down. She wanted to know why there were so many men in the grounds."

"A visit from the police," Carlos replied. "A routine check-up you understand."

"I understand perfectly," Janique said sweetly, and added nothing further until Carlos, with a glance of apology at Stephanie, left the room.

The moment the women were alone Janique's expression changed from meakness to one of hatred. "Carlos is a very clever man," she drawled. "He's got engaged to you just in time."

"I don't understand you."

"Don't you? Surely you know it was the only way he had of keeping you quiet."

Stephanie clenched her hands in anger. "I'd rather you didn't say any more. I know my engagement was a shock to you, but Carlos and I love each other."

"I'm sure you do. At least I'm sure *you* love *him*." The sloe eyes lifted. "Why do you think I came to the Castelo, Miss North? Because of the scenery or because I wanted to see the Condesa! I came because of Carlos and you know it as well as I do. He loved me and he would have married me if you hadn't discovered the turret room."

Stephanie caught her breath. "How do you know? Who told you about it?"

"Like you, I learned of it by accident, but unlike you, I didn't blurt it out to anyone." She paused and admired one long scarlet fingernail. "There's one thing you should know, Miss North. Carlos realized he could trust me to be quiet, but he isn't so certain of you. That's why he asked you to marry him." She paused. "As for me, I will wait until he comes to me. And he *will* come. You haven't a hope of keeping a man like Carlos happy for long. You're too cold, too reserved to give him all he needs." She laughed delicately. "Besides, you're not married yet. As soon as Carlos has returned the rest of the stolen collection he won't have any need to placate you. That is when he'll tell you the engagement has been a mistake."

"You're lying!" Stephanie burst out.

Janique shrugged. "You must think as you like. I'm only telling you the truth for your own sake."

"I don't believe you. And I don't want to hear any more."

Fighting back the tears, she ran from the room. But although she put distance between them it was impossible to put out of her mind all that Janique had said. The story rang too true to be dismissed as a fabrication woven out of jealousy. Carlos's announcement of their engagement had been too precipitate for her to believe that it was anything other than a spur of the moment decision. If he had loved her, why had he asked Janique to stay at the Castelo?

Tears flowed down Stephanie's cheeks and weeping, she flung herself on her bed and buried her head in the pillow. What a fool she had been – what a gullible fool! The only reason Carlos had asked her to marry him was to make sure she did not return to London with Johnny.

Gradually her sobs ceased and, wiping her eyes, she sat up. Carlos must be made to see that he did not have to buy her loyalty by marriage, that he did not have to pretend he loved her in order to keep her silent until he returned all the jewels. No matter what happened she would never betray him, never do anything to hurt the name of Maroc. Cynically she knew she was a fool, knew too that once she had given her love she could never take it back. Time and distance might separate her from Carlos, but nothing would be able to obliterate him from her heart.

Slowly she got to her feet and opened the wardrobe door. Taking out her dresses one by one, she laid them on the bed and began to fold them, her tears marking the material as she placed them carefully in her case.

It was nearly lunchtime when Stephanie went downstairs again. Now that she had come to her decision her one desire was to leave the Castelo as quickly as possible. She would go to the inn and wait there until Robert was able to arrange reservations on the plane. She could not face the thought of seeing Carlos, of hearing him protest his love when she knew he did not mean it. She would try to leave without his knowing: a short note telling him of her decision and her promise that she would never betray his secret would be all that was necessary.

On the terrace a buffet lunch was laid, and her heart thumped painfully as she looked to see if the familiar figure were there. But the terrace was deserted and she sat on a hammock and idly swung it backwards and forwards.

Dinis came through the French windows, permitting himself a smile as he saw her. "The Conde has been looking for you, *senhorita*. I sent Luisa to your bedroom, but although she knocked many times she could get no reply."

Stephanie flushed, remembering her determination not to open the door to anyone. "I must have fallen asleep," she said lamely. "Was it important?"

"The Conde was called away and he wanted to see you before he left."

"How do you mean, called away?"

"For a couple of days, *senhorita*. It was very sudden."

'It certainly was,' Stephanie thought to herself, and wondered what was the reason for Carlos's departure. So her problem was solved after all: by the time he came back she would be many miles away. There was no one to stop her leaving now. The Condesa and Janique would certainly raise no difficulty and neither would Miguel. Grimly she realized that they would all take her word that she would keep silent: all except Carlos. If she had doubted him, so had he doubted her – his proposal of marriage had been proof of that.

She stood up as she heard the tap-tap of the Condesa's stick cross the parquet floor and a moment later saw the frail, black-gowned figure move on to the terrace.

"I didn't expect to see you here already," the Condesa said graciously. "The last few days you've been working so hard we have always had to send word for you."

"I've finished my work now," Stephanie said. "I'm leaving for England today."

"So suddenly?"

"Yes."

"I am glad." The old lady held out a wrinkled hand. "It

would be insincere of me if I were to say anything else, but I know you understand what I mean."

"I understand very well," Stephanie said tonelessly. "But you've nothing to fear from me. Either about the . . ." She paused. "About the jewels or about Carlos."

Carefully the Condesa sat down. "So you know the secret of the Marocs? I suspected you did." The frail voice grew faint and a lace-edged handkerchief touched the pale lips. "It has been a burden I have carried for most of my married life. When my husband died I thought his secret would die with him, but he was determined to bequeath it to his sons. It was a bitter blow to me when I learned that Miguel had inherited more than his father's name. For months Carlos and I pleaded with him, but when we realized it was hopeless, Carlos decided to fight back." The stick fell to the floor and Stephanie bent to retrieve it. Green eyes looked into faded brown ones and the Condesa smiled. "It is difficult to fight silently, yet that is what Carlos did, and now the battle is nearly won. In a few more months everything will be returned."

"Miguel may start collecting again."

"No," the Condesa answered. "Carlos will see to that. He will watch him like a hawk."

"It's not fair," Stephanie said passionately. "Why should Carlos ruin his own life because of . . ." She stopped. "I'm sorry."

"Don't be sorry, my dear. But in a family like ours we do not take our responsibilities lightly."

Stephanie mused on these words as Manoel drove her to the inn. Her farewells had been made hurriedly: to the Condesa, to Dinis and the other servants. She had seen no sign of either Miguel or Janique and had been glad of it. Even now she could not believe that her stormy time at the Castelo had come to an end and that she had actually left it for ever. Peering through the back window of the car, she strained her eyes for a last glimpse of it. "Good-bye," she whispered, and knew it was good-bye to Carlos too.

'We do not take our responsibilities lightly,' the Condesa had said, and had been speaking for Carlos as well; he had even been willing to marry a girl he did not love in order to fulfil his obligations, Stephanie was glad she had spoken to the Condesa this morning, for she knew that the old lady would be able to convince her son that he had nothing to fear from her. Married to him or separated from him, she would never do anything to harm his name.

Resolutely she turned from the window. She must look to the future now and try to put the past behind her, where it belonged.

From her bedroom window Felicity saw the Lagonda parked in the square and ran out to meet her sister. "So you've left." She glanced at the luggage.

Stephanie nodded. "I've left. But don't ask me any questions, Lissa. I was terribly wrong – terribly wrong. It wasn't Carlos—"

"I know all about it," Felicity said quietly. "Johnny came to see me before he went back to London. I wish you could have gone on the plane with him, Stephanie. I'm worried about you staying here."

"You needn't be. The Marocs won't harm me. Carlos knows I'll never tell a soul."

But Felicity still looked worried and, taking Stephanie's arm, led her on to the terrace where Robert was sitting at a table. Stephanie sensed that her sister had already spoken to him, for beyond commenting that she looked tired, he did not mention her precipitate flight from the Castelo.

"I managed to get seats on the plane in the morning," he said, "so by this time tomorrow we'll be home again. And I shan't be sorry either," he added, looking with distaste at his cup. "These foreigners don't know how to make a decent pot of tea."

"Oh, Robert!" Felicity laughed. "Portugal has other things to offer besides tea. You don't travel for things you can get just as well at home. You really are insular!"

"*Me*, insular? What nonsense you talk."

Looking from one to the other, Stephanie detected a comradely quality in their friendly bickering: almost like a young married couple. She sighed. Although at heart she was delighted that Robert was getting over her, she could not help a slight pang at the knowledge. She had got so used to knowing he was there, a reliable 'old faithful' whose affections were as stable as his nature, that she could not help missing them now that he appeared to be withdrawing them.

The phone rang inside the hotel and her heart leapt. Perhaps it was Carlos, returned sooner than he had anticipated, ringing to find out where she was. No sooner had the thought entered her mind than she rejected it. She had finished with Carlos for ever and even if he did call her, she would not speak to him. But when the minutes went by and nobody appeared to ask her to the telephone, she knew an illogical sense of loss.

Felicity pushed her chair back from the table. "I'm going up to pack. What about you, Robert?"

"I've done mine."

"You're always so sensible!" She smiled at him and went into the hotel.

Robert frowned. "Felicity's changed, you know."

"Do you think so?" With an effort Stephanie brought her thoughts away from herself. "In what way?"

"She was always so quiet and sensible. Now she seems much less reserved – less circumspect. Why, if I didn't know her so well, I'd say she was mocking me!"

Stephanie laughed. "Does it matter if she does?"

"Of course not. Why should it? I—" He broke off. "Stephanie . . . Felicity asked me not to say anything to you about Carlos, but I just want to say one thing – you'll get over it. People always do in the end, you know. And when that time comes I shall be waiting for you."

"No, Robert! I don't want you to. I could never love you. Never! Why don't you stop wasting your life and look for someone else?"

"I shall never change."

Stephanie tried to check her irritation. "I used to think Felicity wouldn't change either, but you said yourself how different she is. And if she can alter, why can't you?"

"I don't see what Felicity's got to do with me."

"Don't you, Robert? You're a bit of a fool sometimes, aren't you?"

Before he could reply she pushed back her chair and walked into the inn and up to her sister's room.

Felicity was putting the last of her things into her suitcase.

"There!" she announced triumphantly. "I've finished the packing. Why don't you lie down and have a rest, old thing? You look tired." She indicated a single bed over by the window that had not been there before and Stephanie sank down on it and slipped off her shoes.

"I think I *will* have a sleep for a while – I didn't have much of a rest during the night."

"Perhaps you'll have lunch in bed. I'll come up later on and see how you are."

Felicity tiptoed from the room and Stephanie lay with her eyes shut. But try as she might she could not get Carlos out of her thoughts and, after twisting and tossing on the bed for ten minutes, she gave it up as a bad job and, bathing her face in cold water, sat down by the window.

Robert was no longer at the table on the terrace and presently she saw him and Felicity cross the garden together and disappear through the gate. Sighing, she got up and went slowly downstairs. If only tomorrow were here and they were on the homeward plane. Perhaps once she had left Portugal behind she would be able to put Carlos out of her mind.

She was at the door when the receptionist called after her.

"Miss North, you are wanted."

Stephanie turned. If it were Carlos she would not speak to him! She must not! If she heard his voice again she would weaken. With a singing heart, hardly knowing what she was doing, she walked slowly to the telephone and lifted the receiver.

"Stephanie?"

Her heart leapt and then sank as she recognized Miguel's voice. "Yes," she said. "What do you want?"

"I must see you." His voice sounded excited. "Will you meet me?"

"I can't. I'm leaving in the morning."

"But I've got to talk to you. Be at the bottom of the road that leads to the Castelo in ten minutes. I promise I won't keep you long."

Stephanie hesitated. Miguel was the last person she wanted to see, but he sounded desperately anxious. Perhaps something had happened to Carlos?

"*Please*, Stephanie," he repeated. "You've got to come."

"Very well. But I won't stay if Carlos is with you."

"If Carlos were with me, I wouldn't—" He broke off. "I'll see you in ten minutes then."

"Miguel, wait—" But it was too late; he had put down the receiver.

Leaving the hotel, Stephanie walked slowly towards the meeting-place. It was only five minutes away, but Miguel was already there, the sun flashing on the shiny bonnet of his sports car.

He leaned over and opened the door for her. "You'd better get in for a minute. We can talk more easily in the car."

Reluctantly Stephanie did so and turned to look at him. He was a very different person from the immaculate, debonair young man she was used to seeing. His clothes were creased, his tie was crooked and a lock of hair flopped over his forehead.

"What do you want?" she asked quietly.

Startled as she was by the fierce expression in his dark eyes, his answer startled her even more. "I want to know where the jewels are."

She stared at him in silence for a moment. "Carlos took them."

"I know he did! That's why I'm asking you what he's done with them!"

"How should I know?"

He laughed harshly. "For the future wife of the Conde de Maroc, you are singularly little in his confidence!"

Stephanie went white. "What do you know about that?"

"I know what Janique told me. And I also know what made my gallant brother propose to you – to make sure you didn't talk—"

"Be quiet!" Blindly she started to get out of the car, but before she could do so, he pulled her roughly back into the seat.

"Oh no, you don't! You're not leaving until you've told me what Carlos has done with the jewels."

"I tell you I don't know—"

"Very well then. If you refuse to talk I shall have to make you."

Stephanie opened her mouth to scream, but her cries were drowned in the noise of the motor as Miguel started up the car and roared down the road in a cloud of dust.

Returning from her stroll with Robert, Felicity went up to see if Stephanie was awake. The room was empty and she went into the hotel lounge and then on to the terrace, but there was no sign of her sister.

"I wonder where Stephanie's gone," she said to Robert. "She didn't tell me she was going out."

"For a stroll, probably."

"I shouldn't think so. She said she was going to rest until dinner."

"Don't worry about her. She'll be back presently."

Felicity frowned and picking up a magazine, sat in a deck-chair and started to turn the pages.

Under cover of lighting a cigarette, Robert studied her: her dark hair fell in a curve over her cheek as she bent to the book. Naturally pale, her skin had acquired a faint tan, intensifying the colour of her forget-me-not blue eyes. He frowned. How different she was from the pale, sarcastic girl he had known in London. She seemed to have acquired a new poise, a more adult attitude to life.

He glanced away quickly as Felicity, with an abrupt movement, flung her magazine to the ground and got to her feet. "It's no good, Robert," she said. "I'm worried. It's not like Stephanie to go off without telling me. Those Marocs are dangerous people and I'm afraid something has happened to her."

Robert rubbed the side of his face. "I'll ask in the hotel if she left a message. But I'm sure you're worrying for nothing. Neither of the Marocs are likely to risk their necks by doing any harm to Stephanie."

He went into the hotel and Felicity watched him, a curious expression on her face. Even in her anxiety for her sister, she pondered on Robert's casual manner. A strange attitude for someone madly in love! 'Oh well,' she thought. 'I'm probably being a fool and she's just gone for a walk. Robert's got more sense than I have.'

But when he came out on to the terrace again his face was pale beneath his tan. "The receptionist said he took a phone call for her. It was from a man and she went out immediately she had finished talking."

Felicity gasped. "I was sure it was something like that! Where could she have gone?"

"Perhaps she went back to the Castelo."

"She wouldn't do that. She was only too glad to get away."

Robert shrugged. "You can't tell with Stephanie. She's so crazy about Carlos, there's no knowing what she'll do. And she's obviously gone to meet him somewhere."

"We must *do* something, Robert. She may be in danger. Those Marocs—"

Robert nodded. "We'll go and see them. Come on, we've no time to lose."

It seemed an eternity to Felicity before the ancient taxi that they had hired had chugged its way up the hill to the Castelo. In pidgin English, a few words of Portuguese and many gestures Robert made the driver understand that he was to wait for them, and together they climbed the steps to the Castelo and rang the bell.

The door was opened by Dinis.

"I would like to see the Conde de Maroc," Robert said.

"He is not at home, *senhor*."

"The other one, then – I mean, Mr. Miguel de Maroc."

Dinis gestured with his arm. "I am sorry, *senhor*, but he is away too."

Robert hesitated and Felicity said, "Perhaps we could see the Condesa?"

Dinis opened the door wider. "I will see for you. Wait in here, please."

He showed them into the drawing-room and they waited uneasily until the tapping of a stick heralded the Condesa's approach. She paused in the doorway and looked at them.

"Good afternoon," she said courteously. "What can I do for you?"

Felicity came towards her. "I wondered if my sister were here?"

"But your sister left early this afternoon – immediately after lunch."

"I know. She came to the inn, but now she's disappeared."

"Disappeared?" A puzzled frown came over the Condesa's face. "But why should you think she is here?"

"She received a phone call," Robert explained. "We think it was from one of your sons, and immediately afterwards she left the inn and hasn't returned yet. We are a little worried, you understand, because she had said she was not going out any more today."

The Condesa drew herself up. "If she has gone to meet my son you may be sure she will come to no harm. I really do not see why you have come here."

"We thought she might have come back to the Castelo with him."

"I can assure you that is not the case. I am sorry I cannot help you." The Condesa inclined her head, the gesture indicating as plainly as words that the interview was over.

Realizing there was nothing more they could do here, Robert and Felicity left the Castelo and it was not until the heavy front door had swung shut behind them that they saw that the taxi had disappeared.

"Oh, lord!" Robert groaned. "Now we'll have to walk back. Do you feel up to it, Felicity?"

Listlessly she shrugged. "I couldn't care how far I walked if only I knew what had happened to Stephanie."

"I'm sure she's all right." He took her arm. "You're getting in a state about nothing. Come on now, let's go back and I'll bet you we'll find her at the inn when we get there – probably searching high and low for *us!*"

He gave her arm a squeeze and she smiled at him, grateful for his reassurances. Arm in arm they set off. Felicity's spirits had revived a little and she was almost convinced that Robert was right and they would find Stephanie awaiting them when they got back.

Suddenly she stopped and pressed Robert's arm. "Listen!"

He stood still. "What is it? I can't hear anything."

"Listen," she said again, and in the silence they heard voices raised. Felicity dropped Robert's arm. "I'm sure it's Stephanie! It's coming from over there."

She pointed towards some bushes and together they broke their way through. The voices got louder and they found themselves outside the summer-house.

Running up the steps, Robert tried the door. It was locked and he banged it with his fist. No sound came from inside, but Felicity was more than ever convinced that someone was there.

"Stephanie!" she called. "Stephanie!"

There was a faint scuffling, but no one replied.

Robert tried the door again. "Are you sure you heard voices?"

"Positive," said Felicity, and rattled the handle. "Go on, Robert, break it open."

He hesitated and then shrugged. "Very well. If anyone complains, it's just too damm bad."

He put his shoulder to the door and heaved. Nothing

happened and he tried again. Twice, three times, he pressed his weight against the wood. Slowly it splintered and with one final lunge he broke it open and almost fell into the room.

Stephanie was pushed against the wall and Miguel was standing over her, his arm across her mouth, his face contorted with rage as he saw Robert and Felicity. Without a word Robert lunged across the room and Miguel, releasing Stephanie, rushed forward to hit him.

Silently the two men fought together, as first Robert went crashing to the floor and then Miguel. But the Portuguese was no match for the tall, sturdy Englishman and with a sudden and unexpected blow Robert sent him reeling against the wall and slithering to the floor. Winded, Miguel lay there, hatred blazing in his eyes as Robert wiped the sweat from his forehead and stooped over him.

"If I had my way you'd be behind bars," he said savagely. "And if Stephanie weren't a crazy fool over your brother she'd help put you there." He leaned closer still. "I'm warning you, Maroc, if you come anywhere near Miss North again, I'll go to the police on my own."

Stepping over Miguel, he gave a hand to Felicity and Stephanie and led them outside. Behind a clump of trees Miguel's sports car was parked, and without any hesitation Robert pushed the two girls into the back and took the steering-wheel.

"But, Robert," Felicity protested, "it's not your car."

"I couldn't care less. That swine's given us enough trouble, he can't object to our giving him a little. If I could smash the damm thing for him I'd be delighted." Savagely he let in the clutch and they roared down the drive.

Felicity sat in silence, watching the back of Robert's neck as he drove purposefully towards Cintra. This was a new Robert indeed! Never had she thought him capable of such decisive action.

'Live and learn,' she told herself philosophically, and turned to Stephanie, who was lying with her eyes closed. "Do you feel all right, darling?"

Stephanie sat up. "I'm fine. A bit shaky, though."

"I'm not surprised. When I think what could have happened to you . . ." Felicity shuddered. "What we need is a stiff drink."

Later, sipping brandy in the hotel lounge, Stephanie told them about Miguel's telephone call and her subsequent meeting with him. "I don't know what he was going to do with me if you hadn't arrived," she concluded. "But I can't believe he would really have harmed me."

"Do you think he'll ever find out what his brother has done with the jewels?" Felicity asked.

"I doubt it." Stephanie moistened her lips. "But I'm afraid he might do something to Carlos."

"Good heavens!" Robert set down his glass impatiently. "Can't you think about anything but Carlos de Maroc? I should have thought you'd had enough of the family by now."

Blinking back the tears, Stephanie pushed back her chair and walked out of the lounge, brushing Robert's arm as she did so. He winced sharply and pressed his lips together.

"What's the matter?" Felicity asked.

"Nothing."

"Yes, there is. You've hurt your arm."

"It's nothing." He grinned ruefully. "I think I must have sprained my wrist when I hit that swine."

"Let me see it." Felicity leaned forward to look more closely and saw that Robert's wrist was puffy, the skin already discoloured. "Looks like a sprain to me," she said. "You'd better come upstairs and let me put a cold compress on it for you."

Grumbling at the unnecessary fuss, he nevertheless followed her meekly upstairs and watched as she expertly tied his wrist with a hand-towel wrung out in cold water. Her face, bent in absorption over her task, wore an expression of concern that surprised and touched him and when the bandaging was finished and she lifted her face to his, he lowered his head and pressed his lips on hers. The warm scent of her hair and the softness of her mouth excited him out of his usual reserve, and, catching her close, his kiss became suddenly passionate.

Sharply Felicity pulled away and started to run out of the room, but he was at the door ahead of her, barring her flight.

"Not so fast," he said. "I'm getting a bit tired of having my women run away all the time. What's the matter with me? Have I got the plague or something?"

Felicity glared at him, her expression cold and withdrawn, her voice sarcastic. "For someone who's supposed to be in love with my sister, I think your behaviour leaves a lot to be desired."

"Who says I'm in love with your sister?" The words were out before he had realized what he was going to say, but once said he made no attempt to withdraw them.

Felicity stared at him. "You can't expect me to believe you're not," she said at length. "You couldn't change all that quickly."

Robert strode over to the window and stood looking down into the courtyard for a moment. When he turned round again there was a determined expression on his face and he spoke slowly, choosing his words with care.

"I didn't really mean to say that," he admitted. "But now it's out I realize it's true. I know I'm a bit of a mug, but even *I* can't go on being in love with a girl who's so plainly crazy about someone else. At one time I thought she might change her mind, but I see now that I was wrong." He smiled ruefully, but Felicity, watching him closely, could detect no bitterness in the smile. "I see now that she'll never change."

Her expression softened. "I'm sorry, Robert," she said gently. "Don't mind too much."

Robert looked into her eyes. "The funny thing," he replied slowly, "is that I don't mind at all."

They smiled at one another, then without a word Felicity walked out.

CHAPTER TEN

As they walked across the tarmac to the waiting plane, Stephanie thought the sun had never shone so brightly, the sky never looked so blue and the scents and sounds of Portugal never seemed so enticing. Climbing into the plane, she settled herself beside Felicity and looked through the window for a last glimpse of the country she had come to love so much.

The plane taxied along preparatory to take-off and Stephanie looked back towards the airport. A tall figure was standing there looking towards them and her heart took a downward plunge. Surely it was Carlos! But as the figure turned and walked back into the building, she saw that his hair was fair and his figure bulky.

"Idiot!" she told herself. "For goodness' sake snap out of your day-dreams."

All night she had lain awake, the image of Carlos constantly in her mind and try as she might nothing she could do would displace it. At last she had got up and taken several aspirins, which had eventually brought her a few hours of uneasy sleep, and now she was paying for them by a feeling of heaviness and unreality. She felt Felicity's anxious gaze on her and giving her sister a reassuring smile, took up a book and tried to read.

But it was no good: the words danced before her eyes and made no impression on her mind. How different the outward journey to Lisbon had been. Then she had been filled with excitement and bright hopes for the future. Now she was returning, her job successfully completed but her heart left for ever amidst the grassy slopes and swift-flowing mountain streams of Cintra.

Giving up all hope of being able to make sense of her book, she let it fall in her lap and closed her eyes. Presently she slept and when she awoke, feeling a little better, saw that Felicity had vacated the seat next to her and was beside Robert.

Thoughtfully she watched them in animated conversation and was relieved to find that she no longer felt any pangs of disappointment at losing Robert: only gladness that things were going to come out right for Felicity after all. How she would have rejoiced if only she had not had her own unhappiness to contend with, but as it was, her joy for her sister was tempered by her own suffering.

She sighed and instantly Felicity turned round. "You had a wonderful sleep, darling. We'll be landing in fifteen minutes."

Unable to believe she had slept for so long, Stephanie sat up and peered through the window. Sure enough it was raining and England was below them. The notice to fasten safety-belts flashed on and soon they started to lose height preparatory to landing.

Mr. and Mrs. North were waiting at the airport and in the rush of greetings Stephanie had no time to think. Although her parents sensed some constraint in her, they did not comment on it, beyond remarking that she looked tired and had better have a holiday before starting work again.

Stephanie was grateful for their understanding and though she knew that later on she would have to tell them all that had happened, at the moment the only thing she wanted to do was rest. The thought of her own bed in her own room was paradise. Alone at last and miles away from the foreign land and the alien people with whom she had got so inexplicably involved, she would have a chance of forgetting the man who had taken her heart.

More quickly than she had believed possible, Stephanie picked up the threads of her life again. Discussing the work she had done at the Castelo she was able to divorce it from all emotion and, watching her father's face as he went through the reports, she was glad she had not let him down.

"This job will just about set us on our feet," he said one morning towards the end of her second week at home. "I've already received confirmation from the Conde as well as from those builders in Lisbon. In another couple of months the whole job will be finished and a nice fat profit will go into our account."

"I'm glad," she said with a slight smile. "Now perhaps you'll send me on more jobs for you."

"Any job you like, my dear. There's a tricky one in Southgate that . . ." Mr. North plunged into talk of business, and relieved that they were off the subject of Portugal, Stephanie gave her full attention to what he was saying.

It was not so difficult to put Carlos out of her mind during the day, but at night, lying in her room, his tall, dark figure came to haunt her sleep, to hold her in his arms and press his lips to hers. Many times she awoke and shed bitter tears, knowing that if she could not marry Carlos she would never marry anyone.

There had been no word from him and as the weeks passed the expectancy that she might hear gradually died. If he had loved her he would surely have come to find her. The fact that he had not done so was proof that Janique had been right. For all she knew he might be married to her. Perhaps they were on their honeymoon, basking in the sunshine of Estoril or on the tropical estates that he owned in South America.

But unhappiness, however profound at its inception, cannot maintain its first impact for ever. A tune on the radio, the sight of a tall dark man walking towards her could still bring back the weeks she had spent in Portugal. But as the summer months gave way to autumn and the autumn months to the first biting winds of winter, Stephanie gradually began to forget.

She was busy at her desk one morning when she was told

that there was a gentleman to see her, and she had hardly put down her pen before Johnny Carlton was shown in. Her first thrill of expectancy died and her palms grew damp as she saw his serious face.

"Hello," he said quietly. "Surprised to see me?"

"A little. It seems strange to meet you in England."

"I live in London," he said with a slight smile, and rubbed his hand across his face in a nervous gesture she had not expected from him.

There was an awkward pause and she took up her pencil and toyed with it. "If you've come to ask me—"

"No, no. I haven't come to ask you anything. I merely came to apologize."

"Apologize?"

"Yes. I've been thinking things over for a long time and this morning I made up my mind I'd come and see you. When you're dealing with crooks, Stephanie, you begin to forget what normal people think and feel, but I see now I'd no right to involve you in what I was doing."

She relaxed against her chair. "I'm glad you're not still annoyed with me. I wanted to help you, Johnny, but I couldn't."

"I see that now, and I wanted to tell you there are no hard feelings on my side. I dare say I should have come sooner, but I wanted to wait until I had something concrete to tell you." He stopped and although she longed to question him, she determined to hear him out first. "The jewels have all been returned," he went on. "My insurance company were notified a week ago, so as far as we're concerned the case is now closed."

She breathed a sigh of relief. "I'm so glad," she said. "So glad. I hope Carlos . . ." She stumbled over the name. "I hope Carlos can keep some control over his brother."

"That won't be necessary," said Johnny. "Don't you know what's happened?"

"No." Her eyes widened with fear. "What's wrong? Is Carlos—"

"Miguel de Maroc was killed in a car crash a couple of months ago."

"I see." A picture of Miguel flashed into her mind as she had first seen him: slim, debonair, a young man of charm who had taken the wrong road. Although she mourned for him she could not help being glad that he was no longer able to torment his mother or Carlos.

Johnny came over to the desk. "I can see it's been a bit of a shock for you. I'd no idea you hadn't been told. As a matter of fact, until a little while ago I was under the impression you were still in Portugal with Carlos."

Stephanie put down her pencil and reached for a cigarette. Now that Miguel was dead and the jewels had all been returned, there was no longer any need for prevarication. Haltingly she recounted her conversation with Janique and her subsequent decision to leave the Castelo.

"Carlos and I could never have been happy together," she concluded. "I realized that and so did the Condesa."

"You mean the Condesa thought so and made you agree."

"No, no," she said quickly. "That isn't true. Carlos and I have different cultures and a different background. He couldn't understand my way of life any more than I could understand his."

"Nonsense! When a man and woman love each other backgrounds don't matter."

"When they love each other," she said softly. "But you see, Carlos didn't love me. The only reason he asked me to marry him was to make sure I wouldn't give his secret away."

"I don't believe it. If he felt like that he would have had to marry Janique too. If it were a question of trusting *anybody* with a secret, I'd have chosen *you*."

She longed to believe him and yet the events of the past few months made it impossible. If Carlos had wanted her he had ample opportunity to find her; the fact that he had not done so was proof that she had been right. Suddenly the conversation became unbearable: there were so many things that were better left unsaid. She stood up and came round the side of the desk.

"It's sweet of you to take this interest in me, but I'd rather not talk about it any more."

He shrugged. "If you're going to let pride stand in the way of happiness . . ."

"It's not a question of pride. You told me yourself Miguel had been dead for months. That means Carlos is free to do as he wants. The fact that he's still in Portugal and I'm here should be proof enough."

Johnny ran his hand across his head and a strand of fair hair fell over his forehead, making him look younger. "O.K., Stephanie. If you don't want to talk about it, we won't. I'd only like to feel that it leaves the way free for me. You know I like you and—"

"Johnny, no. Don't say any more. You'll always be associated in my mind with something I'd rather forget."

He was silent for a moment. "You don't mince words, do you?"

She smiled slightly. "It's my red hair."

Without replying he leaned forward and touched his lips to it, then turning on his heel, strode across the room. At the door he paused and turned around. "How's Felicity?"

"She and Robert announced their engagement last week. They're getting married in the spring."

He raised his eyebrows. "Give them my congratulations, will you? I'm glad *that's* turned out all right anyway. At least . . ." He hesitated.

"You needn't be sorry on my account, Johnny. I'm as pleased as they are. As for me," she smiled ruefully, "I'm afraid I'm a one-man woman and that's all there is to it."

"You're an ass," he replied gently. "But I love you for it." He raised his hand in farewell. "So long, Stephanie. We'll meet again one day and perhaps you won't feel the same."

Seeing Johnny again brought back dormant memories, and thinking over the situation, Stephanie was honest enough to admit that in the back of her mind had been the hope that one day Carlos would come to find her, the hope that she had meant something to him after all. Johnny's conversation left her in doubt no longer. If Carlos had wanted to find her there had been nothing to prevent him, and the fact that she had received no word from him was irrefutable proof that she had been right in assuming that his love had merely been pretence.

She had always prided herself on facing facts and with a great effort she determined to resume her old life. Once more she got in touch with her friends, went dancing, visited the theatre, worked long hours in the office. On one occasion Johnny telephoned, but she was adamant in her refusal to see him, and after a further phone call she did not hear from him again. As day followed day new memories began to crowd out the old and she told herself that soon the time would come when she would succeed in banishing the young Portuguese not only from her heart but also from her mind.

But one evening, returning late from the office, the thought of Carlos could not be shaken off. All day she had seen his face before her and now that the day was over and she was tired, he loomed stronger in her thoughts than ever. She dreaded the night of sleeplessness that lay ahead, when she would turn over and over in her mind every word that had passed between them, trying to analyse each gesture, each inflection in the low, husky voice.

Slowly she walked along the road to her home, disregarding the fierce wind that pulled at her coat and the gusts of rain that dampened her hair and left glistening drops on her face. She had grown thinner since her return from Portugal, but the dark smudges underneath her eyes enhanced their luminosity and her thin cheeks threw into relief the delicate bone structure of her face.

As she crossed the road a young man whistled after her and she flushed with irritation. At one time such an expression of admiration would only have amused her, but now she took no pleasure in looking pretty. She wanted only one man's arms, only one man's touch.

Wearily she let herself into the house and flung her hat and coat on the hall settee. Her father came out of the dining-room, his expression concerned.

"I phoned you at the office, but you'd left a long time ago."

"I went along to one of the building sites."

"For heaven's sake!" he said irritably. "That's not the job for you."

"I know. But I wanted to see how they were getting on." She ran her hand through her hair. "Where's Felicity?"

He grinned. "Where do you think? Out with Robert."

She smiled and walked towards the kitchen, but her father stopped her. "You'd better go upstairs and make yourself tidy. There's somebody to see you."

"It must be about my stall at the church bazaar. I'd better get it settled right away."

Before her father could protest she pushed open the door of the sitting-room and walked in. The man by the mantelshelf turned round and Stephanie felt the colour drain from her face.

"Carlos!" she whispered. "What are you . . . what are you doing here?"

"I came to see you." He moved towards her and beneath the bright light suspended above him she saw that he was thinner and paler, his hair more intensely black than she had remembered, his features more hawk-like and stern.

"You had no right to leave the Castelo while I was away," he said gravely. "The least you could have done was to have spoken to me first."

"It's a long time ago." She forced herself to remain calm and was glad that the faintness that threatened to overwhelm her made her voice icy and controlled. "Such a long time ago that I've forgotten."

"Don't lie to me!" His voice was harsh. "Whatever you do, don't lie to me. Do you think I didn't want to come after you when I came home and found you gone? I wanted to catch you and bring you back – make you a prisoner so that you could never escape from me again."

"You took a long time to make up your mind."

"I had good reason for not doing anything. I love you, Stephanie, but when I left the Castelo and I was away from you I realized how wrong I was to expect you to share my life."

"I see." She walked over to a chair and sat down on the edge, careful to keep her hands tightly clasped so that he should not see them trembling. "If you felt that way you were right not to come after me, but you should never have come here now."

"I had to come. I'm free, Stephanie – free!"

"I know. I saw Johnny Carlton a little while ago and he told me everything."

"Then there's no need for me to explain further." He came closer and held out his arms. "Miguel can no longer torment us. All my life is before you, Stephanie, waiting for you to share it with me."

It would be so easy to move into his arms, Stephanie thought, yet it would solve nothing. There were still too many doubts to be answered, too many things left unsaid that could spoil their life together.

"No, Carlos, what you ask is impossible. We can't turn back the clock."

"I don't want to turn back the clock. It's the future I'm concerned with. The hours, the days, the years ahead. So many years," he said passionately.

"I can't!" She pushed back her chair and stood behind it. "It's four months since I've seen you, Carlos. Four months in which I've managed to live without you, to make my life all over again."

"But I love you."

"If you love me you should have come to me sooner. Miguel has been dead for two months, Carlos. What kept you away so long?"

He moved nearer, but seeing the expression on her face, he

shrugged and stepped back again. With the gesture she knew so well and loved so dearly, he reached into his pocket for a cigarette and carefully lit it.

"Like most women you delight in explanation, in analysing every torturing doubt and fear."

"You can't blame me." She was determined not to let him go unanswered. The first sight of him had robbed her of speech, her desire to throw herself into his arms so strong that clear thought had been impossible. Talking to him now, with the distance of the room between them, she knew she must solve the problem. If they had a future together it must be a future with nothing from the past to mar it. If she had to live her life alone she must eradicate him completely from her heart.

"Well," he said, a faint twinge of humour in his voice. "You're looking at me as if you can see the answers to your questions in my face."

"Perhaps I can."

He shook his head. "All you can see mirrored in my eyes is your reflection. All you can see on my mouth is my desire to kiss you. A poetic Portuguese," he mocked. "You can see what you're letting yourself in for."

"I'm not letting myself in for anything. I was under the impression that – that you were already married to Janique."

The breath hissed sharply between his teeth. "So that was in your mind. How could you believe I could ever marry another woman?"

"Why shouldn't I? You were very fond of her."

"There's a difference between being fond and love, but perhaps you're too innocent to know."

She reddened. "There's no need to be insulting."

"Insulting? *Mae de Deus!* What else do you expect me to be? I've come thousands of miles to see you, and all you do is question me. I've never loved Janique. It was you – only you from the first moment I saw you. I don't know what Janique told you or what my mother told you either, but I want you to be my wife. And if you won't I'll never marry anyone else."

He flung his cigarette into the fire. "I didn't come to you immediately Miguel was killed because there were many things I had to do first. As I told you before, I wanted to come to you with nothing left over from the past. The moment all the jewels were returned and the estate was settled I considered myself free."

Listening to his voice Stephanie could no longer keep up the pretence – even to herself – that she was unmoved by his presence. One look from his dark eyes, one touch from his hands and she was solely his. She had known from the beginning that he was domineering, cruel, and listening to him talk she knew that this cruelty and strength of character had kept him apart from her. He had wanted to come to her free – all his problems solved. And if this meant waiting months, it had not served to deter him. She sighed. There was so much about Carlos that would always disappoint and hurt her, yet there was so much about him that she could never find with anyone else.

"Well," he said at last, "my future rests with you, Stephanie."

Without being aware that she was moving, she found herself in his arms.

Tenderly his hands caressed her shoulders and the gentle curve of her breast, his lips warm on hers, moving gently backwards and forwards until her own parted and she gave herself up to the sudden tide of passion that trembled through him.

"Oh, Carlos," she said brokenly. "How can I fight you when I want you so much?"

"There will be many times when you will fight me, *pequena*." His breath was warm on her cheek. "But always it will end like this – in my arms, close to my heart." He moved back and looked into her eyes. "You will have to live with me in Portugal. Will you mind?"

"Wherever you are will be my home," she whispered. "No matter what anybody says I realize now that we were meant for each other."

"As long as you will always remember that, nothing can come between us."

From his pocket he drew out a small black box and, lifting the lid, disclosed a large pear-shaped pearl surrounded by multi-coloured diamonds.

"I returned this to its rightful owner," he said softly, "and persuaded him to let me buy it. I would like it made into a necklace for you."

"The Queen's Tear," Stephanie breathed. "Oh, Carlos, it's magnificent!"

"It is no lovelier than you." His hands were warm on her shoulders, caressing her skin. "I hope this will be the only tear you will ever know."

Mills & Boon Classics

The very best of Mills & Boon romances, brought back for those of you who missed reading them when they were first published.

There are three other Classics for you to collect this February

ISLAND OF PEARLS *by Margaret Rome*
Many English girls go to Majorca for their holiday in the secret hope of meeting romance. Hazel Brown went there and found a husband. But she was not as romantically lucky as she appeared to be – for Hazel's was a husband with a difference ...

THE SHROUDED WEB *by Anne Mather*
For several very good reasons Justina wished to keep the news of her husband's death from her frail, elderly aunt. Then she heard of the Englishman Dominic Hallam, who was in hospital suffering from amnesia, and the germ of an idea came into her mind ...

DEVIL IN A SILVER ROOM *by Violet Winspear*
Margo Jones had once loved Michel, so when he died she found herself going to look after his small son in the French chateau of Satancourt. There Margo met Paul Cassilis, Michel's inscrutable brother, to whom women were just playthings, but in "Miss Jones" was to find one woman who was determined not to be.

If you have difficulty in obtaining any of these books from your local paperback retailer, write to:

Mills & Boon Reader Service
P.O. Box 236, Thornton Road, Croydon, Surrey, CR9 3RU.

Mills & Boon Classics

The very best of Mills & Boon
romances, brought back for those
of you who missed reading them
when they were first published.

and in
March
we bring back the following four
great romantic titles

A SAVAGE BEAUTY *by Anne Mather*
The disturbing Miguel Salvaje married Emma Seaton against
her will and bore her back to Mexico as his wife. There was a
state of perpetual conflict between them, and to make
matters worse Emma found there was another woman sharing
the house with her and her new husband ...

RING OF JADE *by Margaret Way*
On the magical tropical island, Brockway's Folly, in the Great
Barrier Reef, Claire met two men — David who needed her
and Adam who didn't. Claire had come to the island to
escape her emotions — but instead she found them threatening
to overwhelm her completely.

THE INSHINE GIRL *by Margery Hilton*
Della and Venetia were the best of friends, but the glamorous
Della just couldn't help outshining Venetia all the time. But
was Simon Manville right when he assured Venetia that it
was the 'inshine girls' that most men wanted to marry?

LUCIFER'S ANGEL *by Violet Winspear*
When Fay, young and inexperienced, married a sophisticated
film director, and was swept into the brittle, shallow social
whirl of Hollywood, she soon discovered that all too often
there is heartache behind the glitter.

If you have difficulty in obtaining any of these titles through
your local paperback retailer, write to:

Mills & Boon Reader Service
P.O. Box 236, Thornton Road, Croydon, Surrey, CR9 3RU.

Masquerade
Historical Romances

Intrigue excitement romance

MARIETTA
by Gina Veronese

Marietta was the richest woman in Florence — but when she fell in love with Filippo, poor but proud, she discovered that her wealth counted for nothing . . .

It could not recover his lost inheritance, or save them both from danger.

THE REBEL AND THE REDCOAT
by Jan Constant

Events of the Scottish uprising in 1745 apparently proved Anstey Frazer a murderess. Yet, on the long and gruelling journey south to her awesome trial, she found herself increasingly attracted to the Redcoat captain who was her captor . . .

Look out for these titles in your local paperback shop from 8th February 1980

SAVE TIME, TROUBLE & MONEY!
By joining the exciting NEW...

Mills & Boon Romance CLUB

WITH all these EXCLUSIVE BENEFITS for every member

NOTHING TO PAY! MEMBERSHIP IS FREE TO REGULAR READERS!

IMAGINE the *pleasure* and *security* of having ALL your favourite *Mills & Boon* romantic fiction delivered right to *your* home, absolutely POST FREE... straight off the press! No waiting! No more disappointments! All this PLUS all the latest news of *new books* and *top-selling authors* in your own monthly MAGAZINE... PLUS *regular* big CASH SAVINGS... PLUS lots of wonderful strictly-limited, *members-only* SPECIAL OFFERS! All these exclusive benefits can be *yours* – right NOW – simply by joining the exciting NEW *Mills & Boon* ROMANCE CLUB. Complete and post the coupon below for FREE full-colour leaflet. It costs nothing. HURRY!

No obligation to join unless you wish!

FREE CLUB MAGAZINE Packed with *advance news* of latest titles and authors

Exciting offers of **FREE BOOKS** For club members ONLY

Lots of fabulous **BARGAIN OFFERS** – many at **BIG CASH SAVINGS**

FREE FULL-COLOUR LEAFLET!
CUT OUT *CUT-OUT COUPON BELOW AND POST IT TODAY!*

To: MILLS & BOON READER SERVICE, P.O. Box No 236, Thornton Road, Croydon, Surrey CR9 3RU, England.
WITHOUT OBLIGATION to join, please send me FREE details of the exciting NEW **Mills & Boon** ROMANCE CLUB and of all the exclusive benefits of membership.

Please write in BLOCK LETTERS below

NAME (Mrs/Miss) ....

ADDRESS ....

CITY/TOWN ....

COUNTY/COUNTRY .... POST/ZIP CODE ....

S. African & Rhodesian readers write to:
P.O. BOX 11190, JOHANNESBURG, 2000. S. AFRICA